Marrow
and other stories

Quotes appearing in "The Lesson of the Rabbi," reprinted with the permission of Scribner, a Division of Simon & Schuster from I AND THOU by Martin Buber, translated by Ronald Gregor Smith. Translation Copyright © 1958 by Charles Scribner's Sons.

Lyrics from the song "Blessed" reprinted in the story "Final Movement" are included with permission from Paul Simon Music, © 1966 Paul Simon (BMI).

The following stories have been previously published elsewhere, several of them in somewhat different form:

"Marrow," first in *Parchment*, No. 4, 1995-6, pp. 70-75; then in *Vital Signs: New Women Writers in Canada* (edited by Diane Schoemperlen), Oberon Press, 1997, pp. 33-38.

"The Prayer," in *Parchment*, No. 2, 1993-4, pp. 24-36.

"Miniatures: Eight Women, The Day They Turn Forty," first in *Kairos*, No. 5, 1993, pp. 46-54; then in *Wordscape3* (edited by Jackie Manthorne), Scarborough: MTB Press, 1997, pp. 37-46.

"The Lesson of the Rabbi," in *Bridges*, Vol. 4, No. 2, Winter 94/95, pp. 82-95.

"Yosepha," in *Lilith*, Issue 12/13, Winter/Spring 1985, pp. 35-39.

ISBN 1-894020-31-6

Published by Warwick Publishing Inc.
388 King Street West, Suite 111, Toronto, ON M5V 1K2
1424 North Highland Avenue, Los Angeles, CA 90028

Distributed by Firefly Books Ltd.
3680 Victoria Park Avenue, Willowdale, ON M2H 3K1

Cover design: Kimberley Young
Text design: Diane Farenick
Copy editor: Melinda Tate

Printed and bound in Canada

Marrow
and other stories

❋{Nora Gold}❋

W
Warwick Publishing
Toronto   Los Angeles

Contents

Acknowledgements

In the space available, it is obviously not possible to thank all the family and friends who have contributed in one way or another to this undertaking. I will therefore thank here only those who played a direct role in the realization of this book. I extend a heartfelt thanks to:

Warwick Publishing—to Nick Pitt for his enthusiasm and commitment to this project, to Melinda Tate for her thoughtful editorial assistance, to Kimberley Young for her beautiful cover, and to Diane Farenick for her page design

Ruth Nevo, Alice Shalvi, and Andy Kaufman for their helpful comments on parts of this manuscript, and a special thanks to Diane Schoemperlen, who has been teacher, guide, and friend

Lipa Roth, for help with background information

Belle Adler and Melissa Friedberg, for never doubting

Joseph Weissgold, my son, for keeping me at all times connected to the everyday joys of life

And last but not least, David Weiss, my husband, for his support, both practical and emotional, throughout the writing of this book, and for his friendship, strength, and love.

~

Marrow

SHE LOST HER BABY in Hebrew. That is, she lost her baby in a hospital in a foreign language. That is, she can't talk about the death of that baby since it happened in Hebrew, in a language that made no sense. In Hebrew they explained to her what procedures were going to be done to her: "*Achshav anachnu nazrik lach chomer.*" And then an enormous needle, something ridiculous and exaggerated, something from a children's cartoon, descended from the ceiling. And as they were sticking it into her—into *her*, into her vagina—she screamed "What are you doing to me?" And they continued what they were doing, and she felt a cold liquid travelling up inside her, numbing muscles and senses she hadn't known she had, and they answered her impatiently, dismissively, like dealing with a detail, *"Hisbarnu lach, hisbarnu lach"*—louder and louder, as if explaining it louder would help.

They knew she spoke no Hebrew. She had told a bald-headed man with a skullcap at Admissions, a man named Benny, formerly from Brooklyn. And they knew, because she had told them, that she was a tourist, whose baby had exploded, and begun bleeding out of her, unexpectedly, inconveniently, while she was in her hotel, undressing to go down to the pool. But they still explained everything to her anyway, calmly, patronizingly, as though she were slightly retarded. Everyone on some level believes that their own language makes sense to everyone else.

⊷⊜⊶

Lying there, she left her body, which was freezing and filled with death, and she left the Babel babble all around her and clung to words. She remembered that in her purse she still had her Hebrew-English English-Hebrew pocket dictionary. It had told her how to find bathrooms, once Brian had gone home and she was suddenly alone in this language, it had kept her from being taken advantage of by sales clerks giving change. She flipped through: What word did she want? What word could help her? "Get me out of here?" Surely not—she could barely walk, she had nowhere to go but back to the hotel or onto a plane, and neither of these was possible now. She looked up "fetus," a straightforward word, no choices or multiple meanings, not like *"shomer"* which means guard, protect or keep, take your pick, none of which, in her mind, had any relation to each other. Fetus: *Ubar*. She checked it in the Hebrew-English—*Ubar*: Fetus. Further down, she saw the word: *Achbar*. *Achbar*, she read, meant mouse. *Ubar-Achbar*. Inside her lived a mouse, a fetus-mouse. That cold stuff they'd injected into her would freeze it, kill it like those cans of stuff you sprayed on mice at home. Some of these solutions dehydrated the mice, flattening them out like paper, and you found little flaccid mice-skins lying all over your house. Other solutions chased them away with aversive smells, or poisoned them slowly. But, Hannah remembered, this was not Canada. Here they freeze their vermin, even in the womb.

⤙══◉══⤚

They had gone for a drive, two days before this happened. It was the last day they would be together. They were at the end of a two-week holiday, and now Hannah was staying on for a five-day conference, while Brian and Jake flew home. She had insisted they go together to the Old City, at least once on this trip, her first time back in eighteen years.

"I'm aware there's an *intifada*, but don't worry," she told Brian, again. "I know this part of Jerusalem like the back of my hand. I walked it dozens of times the year I was here." Brian was driving but his right eye, the one she could see, had travelled toward her, and she read his anger. He resented her attachment to the past, to the life she'd had here, before him. And the intifada was in full swing, and he didn't...like...risks.

"I won't endanger Jake," he said.

"Of course not!" said Hannah. "For Christ's sake, Brian."

They decided to just drive to the Old City and around it, not stop at all, not get out even once from their yellow rental car. She also promised not to slow him down to point things out all the time. She didn't tell him as they sped past that here King David had built an underground tunnel so the people could still live within the walls while under siege, by draining water from the hidden pool in the valley.

They were proud of themselves for this decision. They were realists, competent. Canadian.

They took a wrong turn, and as they entered the village, Hannah recognized it, remembering how her lover Merom, lanky, tanned, and barefoot, had brought her here to this village nearly two decades before, both of them dangling their sandals from their fingers, indolent from love, from the beach, from love on the beach. They had stopped here on their way back from the sea to visit an Arab guy whom Merom knew from the university, and they sat on the floor with Mohammed and his parents and drank sweet, mud-like coffee. Now as they drove, she looked out towards the left, and was admiring the stands of fruit piled high—figs, dates, pomegranates—and the squatting old men playing a game with sticks, when she saw him. A young man, eighteen or twenty, was running towards them, his hand raised high, and he was spinning something around and around, like a slingshot. "*Hurry!*" she said to Brian. "*Faster.*" But it was too late. She heard the sound of a tire exploding, and turned round to see Jake in his carseat covered in glass and a huge jagged wound in the rear window. Jake stared at her blindly for a moment and then burst into tears. Another stone followed a second later.

They turned right at the fork in the road, her instinct taking them out onto Hebron Street rather than back into the village. None of them, miraculously, seemed hurt. At the police station, a detective and his assistant stared at Hannah's swollen belly and offered her a chair. While Brian took Jake and left to get the car repaired (at the government's expense, under a clause called "Acts of God"), Hannah told the officer what had happened. His spoken English was terrible, but he seemed to understand her. At any rate, he filled out many forms, which took an hour-and-a-half. Later, Hannah made light of the incident for Jake's sake, saying it had been a bad car, but now it was fixed, and there was nothing left to be afraid of. That evening, they drove the car again with the rear window fixed, their last night together, to a restaurant with a hanging garden that they couldn't quite afford.

The bald guy from Admissions, from Brooklyn, drops in to see Hannah. She knows that for Orthodox Jews like Benny, each good deed, each *mitzvah*, scores them a point or two in the world to come, and visiting the sick is a special one, worth three or four points at least, especially when visiting a woman who is alone, without a man. But even so she is happy to see him.

"How are ya?" asks Benny, sitting down on the chair near her bed.

She smiles at him. She wants to tell him that they froze her insides, she wants him to know that now not only is her baby dying, but so is her love of this land, and so is she. But she feels confused now even in English, as though she's forgotten how to speak altogether. She just looks at him.

"They want me to tell you," says Benny, "that it's all going very well. It's taking effect. Soon you'll go into labour."

"Labour?" she says dumbly. "Labour?"

"Yeah, you gotta go into labour to get out the…" He hesitates here, his religious sensibilities alert. Is it a life? Is it a human thing? It may be in God's image, it must not be insulted.

"…my baby," she concludes for him, staring at his skullcap.

"Well, it's not alive, you know," he says, looking away. Hannah feels sorry for him, he is so embarrassed in his errand of mercy. But she feels stupid again, too. She doesn't know what he is talking about.

"My baby," she says like a moron. "My baby's inside."

"It's God's will," says Benny. "You have to accept…"

At home Hannah would have told him to fuck off. She knows from the kind of skullcap he wears, and from a remark she overheard him make, that he is a Jew who believes (in addition to his belief in God) that Arabs are animals, that the only good Arab is

~
13

a dead Arab, and that we are entitled to all the land and all their homes and all the good jobs, and if they behave they can live here and serve us and clean our houses and empty our bedpans. (Yesterday a young Arab girl, no more than sixteen, had emptied Hannah's bedpan. What does it feel like, Hannah had wondered, to be sixteen and to be grateful to have a job emptying other people's excrement?) She knows Benny's politics without their ever having discussed them, and she blames him for everything.

Hannah starts to laugh. Her uterus is frozen, there is a half-dead mouse-fetus stuck inside her, and she is getting all worked-up about politics. At that moment the first spasm strikes. Her face is twisted, half in a laugh, half in the pain of labour.

"Get the nurse," she says.

By the time the nurse arrives, Hannah is sitting cross-legged on the bed, looking into the bedpan. Her baby is the colour of liver, the same red-brown colour as the earth of this land, the blood-drenched land that she tried to make her own. She has failed. It is lying on its side, and its embryo arm, too skinny, is bent at the elbow, as if sleeping, and the hand has already begun to separate from the arm. A branch, but a broken one. It is her baby and she longs to pick it up and hold it; but it is a dead thing and it repulses her. With one finger, she reaches out and strokes its upper arm, and it is clammy, like touching meat, but warm, like the warm places in her own body. She shuts her eyes and nods and the nurse takes it away.

As she drifts into sleep, unexpectedly the nonsense babble around her begins to make sense. The woman in the bed next to Hannah is telling her husband that she loves him; the nurse is complaining to somebody about her long hours; and a woman farther down is sobbing, and between the sobs Hannah hears the phrase over and over "a curse, a curse on us all." All women's voices, the voices of other almost-mothers, all bleeding, all with empty, aching uteruses. In her half-state she realizes that now she understands Hebrew again, it has all come back to her. But what she understands, somehow, is another language altogether. It is the language of the body that she lived in back then, when she first learned Hebrew, when she first had her body loved, when she first felt the soft marrow inside her own bones and heard the strumming drumming streaming of her blood. She has forgotten all this in her married years: the language of desire and loneliness, and more loneliness, and more desire.

The Prayer

SHE IS ONE OF only five people at her *shul* who can lead the High Holyday services, and the only one out of these five prayers who is a woman. She sits in the front row and awaits her turn. The man who is currently leading rushes through the introductory prayers, mumbling long passages in an incomprehensible monotone, and periodically looking up at the clock as if racing against time. Laura tries to restrain her annoyance. After all, this is not a day for anger, for rebellion: Today is Yom Kippur, the holiest day of the year, the day on which one's fate is decided—"who shall live, and who shall die." One can try to tip the balance, of course, with prayer, and charity, and deeds of kindness during the ten preceding days, but Laura hasn't bothered. And even today, on

~

the final day for soul-searching, for repentance, she still resists. She has had a bad year, and has no energy left over for thinking about her and God, plumbing her depths, reflecting on body and soul. God has done what God has done, she has done what she has done. She presumes they both have done their best.

The morning prayers, the ones she is about to sing, are the ones that once she loved the most. She loved the morning, when the day was still fresh, the time before anything bad had happened yet. She used to feel, leading prayers, like a robin on a branch, warbling brightness and joy; and somehow she was able to magically infect the listening congregants with her chirpy shining love of the world. But today she will not warble, today there is no freshness. She feels dirty: On Yom Kippur it is forbidden to wash; and in the hot room she can feel the sweat on her body and smell her own sour smell. She smells also of Burt last night (and that too is forbidden on this day). After they ravished each other, she refused to shower, asking him belligerently, "Why add insult to injury?" He laughed at her savagely, said he liked it when she got pious on him. Then he quickly showered and went home to his wife and son.

Automatically, without thought or intention, Laura is responding to the prayers: "Amen," "Blessed be God," "Blessed be God and God's name," "Amen." She can feel, through the eyes sliding in her direction, the other women's approval, their recognition of her. Some of them even smile at her respectfully, or nod. She knows how she looks to them: *A Woman of Knowledge*. A philosophy professor; someone who knows the right responses at each point in the service without even having to look at the *machzor*, the High Holyday prayer book; and the only woman able to lead the service. In these times of feminist hope, this is nothing to sneeze at.

But of course they don't really know her at all. Her admirers are a lawyer, a psychoanalyst, and a film-maker. The psychoanalyst is wearing a ridiculous hat with a large purple plume. She looks for all the world like the Cat in the Hat, the character in the children's book and the beloved imaginary playmate of Laura's childhood, who comes in times of boredom, wreaks havoc, breaks all the rules, and restores order only at the very last moment before Mother returns. Laura realizes she must have been staring because the psychoanalyst flashes her a big smile and wiggles two of her fingers in a wave. Laura, embarrassed, looks away.

She tries to listen to the man who is leading. *Good God,* she thinks, *what a butchery.* She may not believe much of anything any more, but still she has some respect for the prayers. How, she wonders, can one mumble-race through words like "God, the soul you have given me is pure...You have breathed it into me," or melodies that long to be lingered over, that melt as sweet as chocolates on the tongue. As if these prayers were not the language of the soul of an entire people, sung year after year across centuries, across millennia, like wooden carts rolling over fertile fields, leaving deep, freshly ploughed tracks.

These prayers once meant something to her. In another life, when Michael was alive, Laura sat patiently at the kitchen table each night after supper, practising, while he lay half-listening on the couch, flipping through the sports pages. She learned the Yom Kippur melody, sung only once a year, as if learning a great secret, entering a secret society which until only recently was forbidden to women, and where every wisdom must be passed in whispers, treasured, held to the heart. Occasionally Michael interjected with a comment, his feet raised and crossed on the arm of the couch. He thought it "neat" that Laura was doing this; he accepted it in his good-natured, easy-going way, his loose grin sprawled over everything, over their whole life together. His quiet warmth, like his long lazy body, was something you got used to, something you couldn't imagine life without: as natural as joking, as stroking, as warm coffee and milk in the mornings brought to her in bed. Sometimes he fell asleep on the couch like a lanky teenager, to the sound of her chanting the strange old tunes.

⊷━◉━⊷

Laura rises and goes toward the back room. On the way she passes the women, and the Cat in the Hat reaches out a limp sweaty hand which Laura briefly clasps, avoiding the pitying eyes. As she continues walking, she hears them whispering behind her that this is her first time back since Michael's death a little over a year ago. "So young. So brave," etc. In the back room, she goes to the east wall, as naturally as if a year hasn't passed, as if things are still the way they used to be, when she came back here every few months, lifted the *kittel*, the special robe of the prayer, from the old brass hook, and donned it slowly and with dignity. The room now doubles as a playroom, and the children on the floor are playing checkers and Scrabble as intensely as if these will decide their fate. The teenage babysitter is over in the corner preparing a snack for the children too young to fast, and she sneaks a chocolate cookie into her mouth on its way from the package to the plate. Laura watches her chomp on it happily while pouring the apple juice into little paper cups. The girl flushes when she turns around with the juice and cookies and notices Laura, but Laura lowers her eyes, pretending not to have seen, and turns toward the *kittel*. A smile plays on her lips, though; it cheers her, somehow, this transgression, so human, almost likable. She feels a sudden bond with this teenager with the stringy hair, whom she has never seen here before. She almost wants to wink at her: a co-conspirator, a partner in crime.

~
20

The children jump up for their snack, and Laura shrugs herself into the communal *kittel* and ties it around the waist. It is white, signifying the gown of one's wedding and the shroud of one's death. These two opposing images, the subject of much rabbinical commentary, do not seem strange to her at all. She has always mixed up weddings and funerals, calling funerals weddings and weddings funerals, ever since she can remember. More precisely since she was seven, when her grandmother died at the first wedding Laura ever attended, falling down the stairs at the *shul*, and dying within minutes (an old woman in a black dress) of a heart attack. Laura's uncle, a doctor, whose wedding it was, tried to resuscitate her, breathing from his mouth into hers to bring her back to life. She remembers her uncle's mouth on her grandmother's, and when he stood up, when even he could see there was no use trying any more, his face was white and filled with horror, and his mouth was smeared with her red old-lady's lipstick. She understood it at the time as a sleeping beauty story where the beauty didn't wake. The grown-ups were completely at a loss—screaming and weeping—and someone was rushing around with a hypodermic needle, stabbing the other grown-ups "to calm them down." Upstairs, the musicians didn't know what was happening, and the wedding music played on.

"We're not going to not marry because of your grandmother," Michael said one day with uncharacteristic sharpness, after four years of waiting for her. They did marry soon after that, but throughout the whole ceremony Laura was rigid with fear, misinterpreted by some present as a clichéd fear of commitment, fear of the married life. She couldn't take her eyes off her father, certain he would clutch his chest, turn white, and fall to the floor like her grandmother. Nothing happened. But at Michael's funeral, after throwing the earth on his coffin, as she walked toward

~

the car down the aisle formed by the two straight lines of funeral guests, she found herself humming the tune that they had made the theme song of their wedding and taught to all the guests: the prayer, "Bless us, Father, together as one."

"For Christ's sake, Laura, be quiet," said Burt, Michael's best friend, walking by her side, holding her elbow. She was singing it loudly and proudly as though walking down the aisle at her wedding. She stared at him for a moment in shock. She didn't know she'd been singing. She hadn't realized that she'd been praying to be "together-as-one" again with Michael, dead with him in the ground.

⊷═◉═⊶

Laura, robed in the *kittel*, leaves the playroom and returns to her seat. *I'd better prepare for my performance*, she thinks. *Because that is what it will be.* She has no faith any more, she believes in nothing since Michael's death—certainly not the possibility of influencing her own fate, of begging or bribing her way to safety. (*If I'm a good girl and fold down the biggest flap on my donation card, then I'll be "inscribed in the good book of life": no death, no loneliness for the coming year.*) She is here only because she promised to come, because last month, after three phone calls, she gave in to the urging of Ted, the president of the *shul*, and agreed to lead this morning's prayers. But she hasn't prepared at all, she hasn't even glanced at the *machzor*. She's assumed it will come back to her when she needs it, like riding a bike, that she can rely on having done it six times before. She reaches out her hand and lifts the *machzor* from the rack in front of her, brushing it automatically with her lips on its way to her lap. Then she opens it.

To her horror, none of it looks the least bit familiar. Not the Hebrew, not the English: The words make no sense to her at all. Then the letters begin to move on the page, and as she stares at them, they bow to her like the Cat in the Hat: gallantly, deeply, dangerously. *It must be the fasting*, she thinks, *I'm losing my mind.* The letters begin to dance. They extend elbows to each other, they twirl and do-se-do, they exchange partners. Next they form into straight lines, each line makes a word, and then trading begins between the words. *Light* trades its "l" for an "n", making it *night.* Night light. A light night. Didn't Maimonides write about this? She remembers something vaguely. *Dat* (knowledge) became *edat* (community), just by switching the *daled* and the *ayin*, giving "knowledge" another layer of meaning, pointing to its deeper truth. The rabbis knew this: That the order of the letters is random; the secret meaning of a word lies buried in its core.

Laura looks more closely at the words on the page.

> *Grief*, she sees, contains *fire.*
> *Scared* and *sacred* are the same.
> *Love* and *evil* are only one letter apart.
> But *evil* is the same as *vile.*
> And *evil* is the same as *live.*

She laughs aloud. A few eyes turn in her direction. She looks down piously, as though praying. Should she go further? Should she go on?

Sure, she thinks wildly, *Why not? I can no longer pray; but at least I can play.* Randomly she selects words off the page. Word-pairs, because she and Michael were a pair. Because even now, after a year, she still can't bear to be alone. But she picks pairs not like her and Michael (harmonious, converging, making sense) but word-pairs like her and Burt (opposing elements) that rub against each other, flint into fire, and yield light:

> *Torah lost*   *Laura tossed*
> *ashes love*   *lashes of*
> *body mind*   *muddy bind*
> *free why?*   *we fry*

She laughs again, unaware this time of the looks she is attracting, and does a few more. But now the words of the *machzor* have begun to mingle with other words, with her own words, from her thoughts and memories. She feels angry, irreverent, alive.

> *pain kiss*   *Cain piss*
> *lark dust*   *dark lust*
> *cancer holy?*   *answer slowly*
> *Michael soon*   *cycle moon*

Laura stops, looks at the clock.

Only minutes have passed. But it seems longer, and she is panting a little, as though she's run a race. She looks around the room. Everything in it seems the same as before: the congregants sitting passively in their seats, and the tuneless, toneless droning from the podium. Soon it will be her turn. She thinks now she'll be able to manage the prayers.

A hand is extended to her; she looks up, and takes it. In spite of herself, she is moved: Ted, a kind man. Although they've spoken on the phone, the last time she saw him face-to-face was a little over a year ago at the *shiva*. In her first week of mourning, he came to her home almost every day to comfort her, often bringing food—a curried chicken dish she recalled, that his wife had made. It was tasty the first time she ate it, less so the second. After a week of this chicken curry, she swore she'd never eat it again as long as she lived.

The *shiva*: She remembers feeling nothing, just a dizzy giddy feeling, the same way she feels now from the fasting and the spinning words. Until it was drawing to its end: On the seventh day, following the morning prayers, she was gripped by panic, by terror as unscalable as a vertical wall of glass. Her house, for seven days full of people, would now be empty; she would be, for the first time since Michael's death, alone. Everyone was already gone but Burt. He and Michael had been frat brothers at U of T and like real brothers ever since; and only his grief equalled, or approximated, Laura's. They were left alone after all the other people had wolfed down the lox and bagels, and said their sincere but relieved good-byes. ("A pity there are no children," people kept whispering to each other, as if she couldn't hear. "It would be a comfort to her, take her mind off herself. But they waited so long. You know, her *career*...")

She and Burt sat in silence on the low chairs; and then when Burt rose, he said in a choked voice, "I hate to leave you," and she stood up and leaned against him and they held each other. He had stayed by her side through everything: He was the one, not her father, not her brother, who held her hand as they lowered Michael's coffin into the ground; who growled at the people to leave her alone, to stop grabbing at her, and to make way, as she turned away from the grave and sang her way, Ophelia-like, down the aisle. Now they felt for each other, and she clung to him, he kissed her cheeks out of tenderness and grief; and it hadn't felt wrong at that time—only later, when he began coming over regularly, and it became a routine: Tuesday evenings, the night that Frances teaches late. It has changed on them somehow: tenderness, shared love for Michael, gone terribly wrong, twisted into its opposite, into betraying him, into defiling the friendship and the love.

And worse than that, harder still to understand: She has never felt such desire in all her life. So unlike the quiet love with Michael, this raging passion, this side of herself she had known nothing about. A need so intense, it tears her from her own mind, from her ability to think, to talk, to smile in a normal everyday way. Last week, she was sitting at her desk at work, reliving the night before with Burt, when she heard a knock at her door. She knows how she must have looked to the poor student standing there. She has seen this face of hers in the mirror: white, torn ragged, haggard with desire. "Did I disturb you?" asked the student anxiously, seeing that face, as Laura tried quickly to fix it; but it was no use. She couldn't. It was stuck on like a mask. The student left, promising to return.

There is no longer any pretense: Tuesdays Burt comes over, throws his jacket on the chair, and they go straight for each other, mouths clinging, lips and breath and tongues entwined, like saving a life—"To save a life is to save the whole world"—and the rest just follows while their mouths stay glued. She clings to life, she claws at it with her fingernails. She will wrest from it its secret, tear out its heart and swallow it slithering like an oyster, to keep up the beating of her own frail heart. This is how it is with Burt: furious, elemental, insistent. Loveless but something as strong as love.

No, Laura decides, shifting in the pew, crossing her legs. *I will not give this up*. She doesn't care that it's Yom Kippur and she is supposed to give up her body to find her soul. Her body is all she has left. Everything she feels now, everything she knows, runs through her body and into sex, like a current running through a river and into the sea. At first she felt guilty about this. In the months after Michael died, she sometimes woke up at night and saw his face before hers; and in the morning, she would vow to break it off with Burt. But now she no longer makes these promises—to Michael, to herself, or to God. Instead, she has recently published an essay, praised as "groundbreaking," entitled

"Moral Ambiguity In Our Time." She could never have written this paper a year ago, before anything was ambiguous: when good was good (and *she* was good), and evil something unknown. Her essay concludes: "For who of us can ever break with life? With the only living branch within reach? That branch that contains everything, till the thaw of spring?"

∘━◉━∘

The introductory prayers are almost over. Laura watches the praying man. A praying mantis, that's what he looks like, with his long insect neck and the little round head on the top. A lower form of life: a creature with no music in him, and no love of words—a creature of no ambiguity. A man who is doubtless, faithful: who has never tasted bacon, or the breasts of anyone but his wife. *But oh!* thinks Laura, *the dullness, the worthlessness, of virtue untried!*

Now he has finished and there is silence in the *shul*. The man turns around, craning his neck in all directions as he looks for Laura; and when he finally spots her, he signals to her emphatically, almost with anger. She rises stiffly and ascends the stairs, shaking his hand without looking at him as they pass.

Up on the podium, her back is to the people, and all she can see before her is the closed ark containing the holy Torah. *What am I doing up here?* she wonders. *Who am I to lead the people? I, who believe nothing...*She pulls the *kittel* tighter around her, and stares, as though they will help her, at the ten commandments inscribed on the tablets above the ark—the same commandments she wore for years around her neck, a gift from her grandmother, until she broke the chain. Again the fasting madness strikes: Floating vaporously in front of the tablets, she sees the face of her childhood rabbi. He floats down towards her and whispers into her ear: "'You shall do, *then* you shall hear.' Jews act first. We are not

Christians who need faith before we can act. We do. And faith will come later, if at all."

If at all. How amazing to think that this might be all right, that others before her have also faithlessly led the congregation in prayer. She thinks of all those who have worn this *kittel*, some of them maybe no better than she. Perhaps some of them, like her, also felt ridiculous praying when there's no one to hear. She feels a little lighter than before. She takes a deep breath. *Don't think. Just do. Open your mouth. Sing.*

She opens her mouth and sings. She begins with the wordless opening melody, singing in a normal voice, just an everyday voice, as though she were humming Yankee Doodle in the shower. Though of course what she is singing is different; she can sense this, she can feel its power creeping up on her, even while she tries to ignore it. These are old, cracked tunes, antique and fragile as vases, but very strong. They can tolerate her flippancy, her indifferent holding of them. She looks at them, looks them over, as she meets them again.

Then words join the music, and she goes on singing in a clear ringing voice, about angels, and holiness, and God. Now the words begin to enter her, and the melody is weaving its way in through her ears, in one, out the other. She picks her way carefully, cautiously, like approaching a tiger, gentling it, circling it, sizing it up. Yet in spite of herself, in spite of her lack of belief, the prayers move her; and by the time she reaches the beginning of the *Sh'ma*, she has become a cantor, swaying to the music. She has become half-man, because all the cantors she's ever seen have been men, swaying forwards and backwards, their bodies rigid, their legs glued together as instructed. But always a part of her remains a woman, too, and she sways side to side, or in circles. She would say that she can't dance and never was graceful, but when she doesn't know she is moving, she hypnotizes with her rhythm and grace. The prayers fill her body. They have become the language of her breath: They have entered her hips, and knees, and shoulders, her thighs, and waist, and head. All of her is swaying now.

Then what always used to happen to her happens again, in spite of who she has become, in spite of what she has learned about herself, despite how she has betrayed Michael, the only man she has ever loved. The prayers take her deeper, and deeper, until by the time she reaches the *Amidah*, the central prayer, she is in the centre of her soul and could no more speak about normal things (like telling the congregation to rise or be seated) than she could pull out a vacuum cleaner and begin hoovering the podium. There are directions about this to the prayer leader: Not to speak while leading prayers, not to separate your legs except when stepping back and forth for the silent *Amidah*; kiss your prayer shawl at each of these points; bow at all of these, but always make sure you are standing upright, with legs together, for the word "God." These instructions—which eight years ago, fearful of making mistakes, she laboriously memorized—are now etched on her body. She is no more aware of them than she is of the gradual change in her voice: It has deepened, it has become powerful, like a tiger stretching. It is no longer her voice, it is the voice of her people.

The rest of the prayers she leads in a trance. She has no real awareness of what's around her, she turns the pages of the *machzor* but sings most of the prayers with her eyes closed; and at the end, when it is suddenly finished, and she is supposed to leave her place and walk up to the ark, she is white and stunned, and trembling. Somehow she manages to get there, and the congregation remembers now, from all the times this has happened in the past, that she always needs help at this point in the service. As she stands, confused and helpless, before the open ark, Ted rushes over, reaches inside the ark, lifts out the *Torah* from its dark interior, and places it in her arms. She stares at it, cradles it, amazed that it has happened again, that something still means something to her, that something still remains of who she used to be. When she carries the silver-gilded *Torah* around the room, to be kissed like a baby by the gentle touch of prayerbooks or the silky threads of prayer shawls, many people smile at her or whisper to her how beautiful her singing was. Some even try to do a little socializing, whispering, "So nice to see you back, Laura. Do you have somewhere to break the fast?" But she can't understand them very well, there is a fog between her and everybody else, and she cannot form her mouth into a smile. Where she is there are no smiles. She has heard that in scuba diving the first thing you learn is how to surface slowly, so as not to burst your lungs by racing too quickly up from the depths to the sunny surface of the water. Maybe the cantors lived in the depths all the time, or halfway up; she can't imagine that they sang these songs from anywhere but the bottom. And it's a long trip up.

For fifteen minutes at least, she sits trembling in her seat, smiling wanly, painfully, to those who rush over and take her hand. Some people say they were "moved." Others kiss her and call her an angel, and she still feels a pounding in her head the way she did when she bounced on her heels three times for "Holy Holy Holy," and on the last one felt herself springboarded upward, her head aiming like a cannonball for the two tablets over the ark. A few people evaluate it as a performance, with words like "stellar" and "triumphant." But as soon as she can, Laura hurries off by herself, down the stairs and out the door.

Outside on the stoop, Laura leans back her head, shuts her

eyes, and cools her face in the strong cold wind. Something has eased in her, something she can barely name. But she feels lighter now, and for the time being at least, some of the terrible deadness in her is gone. She stands slightly trembling, vibrating like a violin string continuing to resound; and as though she's been tuned to a higher pitch, she feels incredibly, wonderfully alive. She feels open now, like a string waiting to be played.

Laura raises her head, looks down the street, and then turns her face slightly to catch more of the wind. The wind plays upon her, gently breezy at first and then with a harsh whiff of autumn warning. She does not flinch; just shuts her eyes, opens herself to it, and feels the moment, the incredible joy of being alive. She stays there for a while, feeling; and by the time she opens her eyes, ready to go back inside, she has the wondering look of a young girl surprised by her very first kiss.

Miniatures:

Eight Women, The Day They Turn Forty

1.

It is not fashionable, it is not politically correct, in the circles in which she moves, to admit this; so she will whisper it:

I love my husband.

I love the way he touches me, I love the way he talks to me, I love it when he whispers to me and strokes my shoulder while he tells me jokes, and secrets, and tender things. I love his sexiness which makes me want him, but it makes me afraid of losing him, but that only makes me want him more. I love his hardness, his realness, his refusal to spend time with people he doesn't like; and the way he mows through problems like other men mow the grass. I love that he calls me his queen and

~

built me a palace. *That he is old-fashioned and romantic, and brought me a dozen roses, red and long-stemmed, today for my birthday. And that other times, for no particular reason, he brings me stupid little things off garage sale crates, like bath oils with sprigs of tarragon inside, that—delicate and pretty as they are—require a crowbar and an electric drill to break through the hippie wax on the top.*

A man who doesn't lie to me, who doesn't say I look like a centre-fold, but who still longs for me. Who lies on the bed waiting while I undress, and watching me, goes hard as a rock. Who wants me so much he can only frown, as if he's trying to remember something but can't remember what, and reach out for me with both his hands.

2.

A toilet full of blood. In it floats something small and crescent-shaped, a shrimp in a small red sea. Something you might find in a restaurant in a sauce.

Her third dead baby, one born every spring.

She looks out the window, away from the toilet, from the blood, from the baby. The nausea rises in her throat.

Outside she sees it is spring: birds, sunshine, hope. Trees full of sap. Birds full of song.

To grab onto something, anything (something pleasant), she wonders what springtime feels like, *real* spring, spring without a baby to mourn. She can't remember. She tries to imagine a spring without blood surprising her on underwear, on the floors of restaurants, filling up toilets. She can't. Springtime now is the time that babies die: It is life hanging by a thin bloody thread, and then unravelling like poor knitting. It is the time that cherry blossoms turn brown around the edges and gracefully float to the ground.

It's all right, she decides, *it really is, that it should always be in the spring, if that's the way it has to be.* But then she adds, ever judicious, ever fair (her grandfather was a judge, after all; she always sees both sides):

Then let spring itself also die. Buds on the tree, never open. Sap in the maple, never flow. Bird never fly, let your wings fall off. Let everything die, like my baby, who's dead this spring for the very third time.

The sparrows scatter before her eyes, their wings beat frantically as they flap themselves upward into flight; and at the same time she hears a loud explosion like the shattering of glass. The window she has been looking through is broken, there is a senseless gaping hole in the middle, and in it sits a hand, as surreal as Magritte's, slowly spreading blood. She feels a new sensation: a pain so sharp it is pleasure, like the burn of a very deep truth. It takes a few moments until she recognizes, with surprise, her own hand in the window, bleeding.

3.

She doesn't know how she fell in love with him, but she did. She fell in love with his soft white hair and the intelligent powerful hands moving eloquently as he spoke; but mostly it was with his deep desire, which drove him to constantly seduce, and steamed through his friendliness like the heat of the earth through summer grass. When he went home, she wrote him long letters that came curling out of her, page after page, like clinging vines. She wrote him everything she thought and everything she felt, speaking to him as if his face were the face of her innermost soul. She was as naively sure of him as a young girl who is insanely inanely in love for the very first time.

His letter, when it came, was direct and to the point. He liked her, she was charming etc., but no, he didn't love her. He didn't feel that way about her at all. She read and reread his letter, biting her hand till it bled.

She decided to get over him as quickly as possible. All that this involved was ripping out what was now the core of her life and then waiting to see what was left. What was left was a gaping hole in her entrails as if a cannonball had ripped through her and left her staring, with her mouth hanging open, at what used to be her stomach. She's seen that somewhere in a World War I movie: a young man, a boy really, lying like that in a field. He died, of course. She tells herself that wounds from love are a metaphor; and if they are only a metaphor, a thing of the imagination, then they cannot be fatal. She reminds herself often that these wounds cannot kill.

She no longer sleeps: At night she leaves her airless room and wanders the cool summer streets. She walks incessantly—uphill, downhill, through streets and gardens; sometimes she walks until the sun comes up, watches it rise from the edge of town. The feel of his kiss comes back to her as she walks, without her volition repeating itself, like a song that plays over and over in your head. One kiss in particular has been etched into her flesh, like the deep groove dug into a record on a favourite song; and her flesh sings this kiss over and over again, like a mantra. She feels, like a broken record, the trembling of her whole body as she puts her lips on his; his initial surprise, and then his answering, demanding tongue.

She talks out loud to herself, past locked-up stores, past staring strangers, explaining: "He doesn't love you. He never will. Not as long as you live. Never." She tells herself this as if trying to make herself believe, or understand, it—as if a little pain now will prevent greater pain later on. Yet even this little bit, when it seeps in, is enough to bring her to a standstill in the middle of the sidewalk, groaning aloud. Today she is forty, she is still lonely, she has walked forty years in the desert, and she thinks she will go mad.

Madness as benign as walking the streets at night, talking to herself like one of the bag ladies in the instant tellers of banks. But madness can also be smiling in a park on a sunny summer day, feeling loved by a man who you know doesn't love you. Or it can simply be clutching at a hole in your stomach, pressing fingers into the wound to stop it from bleeding, when anyone with half a brain can tell you there isn't any hole there at all.

4.

All she wants is to float, thoughtless and weightless, like a piece of driftwood. But she doesn't mind acting like an adult at her job, carefully filling test tubes with chemicals so toxic that the slightest spill would mean the disappearance of half her hand before the acid could be stopped. She wears a white lab coat and is widely respected for her work. Last year she won the International Chemistry Prize in Geneva, and her trophy sits collecting dust on the shelf with her test tubes. She doesn't mind her professional success. She also doesn't mind dressing up for her boss—an old man—in a little black dress and high heels and pearls, making him proud in public; or at other times in all sorts of strange and kinky outfits, exciting him in private.

But really she's only a little girl: four, not forty. A girl who grew up in an orphanage. (In the interviews that followed the prize, no one ever asked her: "Did you grow up in an orphanage?") Tonight they will go out for dinner to celebrate her birthday. Discreetly, because his wife is in an asylum, and this relationship of theirs—so much more than esteemed colleagues and

~

37

collaborators—is still only an open secret. He will take her to an expensive French restaurant (he will order the wine, he will pedantically explain to the waiter *exactly* what he means by "rare"); and she will be his good girl: sophisticated, *charmante*, as seductive as he is in the mood for, she will laugh at all his jokes. After dinner, at her apartment on the 26th floor (white carpet white furniture), they will do their sex things, whatever he wants, and afterwards he'll laugh an embarrassed laugh, and blush, and gratefully thank her, as always.

But then she will pretend to be sleepy, and she'll lie in his arms, and he will hold her, which is all she really wants. When he holds her like that, she feels like a baby: a contented, sucking baby—*imagine being loved just because you're born.* She is careful not to let him know, as careful as not spilling acid-based chemical on her hands, that this is all she wants. She will act as if she is just sleepy, that she has slipped into this half-state in his arms because he has made her so happy—with sex, or his gifts, like the diamond tiara he presented to her on her last birthday, watching her face closely as she opened it, and beaming when she smiled.

But of course such things don't matter to her in the least. All she wants is to lie, curled-up and comforted, in his affection and his warmth. She wants to be carried like a raft at sea. She wants to float.

5.

She dreams at night of butterflies: colourful, flitting restlessly from branch to branch, tree to tree, easily spotted among the dark green leaves. (Men are naturally attracted to her, but even when they love her she won't marry them, saying she doesn't want to be pinned down.) Lately she dreams of butterflies nailed to exhibit plates in museums, crucified through the wings.

She awakens nauseated, unable to eat breakfast; and even later in the day, the dream still dreaming inside her, she has no appetite. Recently she has lost a lot of weight very quickly: Five pounds, ten, fifteen, twenty, like the counting song she skipped to as a child. Her body began to disappear: Her breasts fell away, then her hips, and finally her woman's shape, the contour of breast, waist, thigh. Now she is small and light and spare, like a girl, or a butterfly. To her surprise, everyone she sees congratulates her, saying she looks fantastic, she's never looked better. Women add in a whisper: "What's your secret?" She stares at them, tempted to tell.

Over the last few weeks, in the month leading up to her birthday, one of the butterflies in her dream has turned into a butterfly-girl, who is being held down by a big feathered vulture. He is pinning her down by her wrists. She struggles as best she can: She squirms and worms and wriggles like a furious little animal; but she is just too skinny and too small, and she doesn't stand a chance against him. He laughs at her as she struggles because he likes her fiery spirit, but also because he is twice her size and can do with her whatever he wants. To him it is just a game.

She would answer these women that she has lost all this weight because she is nauseated by her dreams: They have destroyed her appetite, they are eating her alive, the way a silkworm growing its cocoon must systematically devour its host, the mulberry leaf. But really that's not it at all. She wants to be twelve years old again, slim and spunky like she was back then. She wants to do it over again and this time do it right: defend that girl, with the will and the talons of a forty-year-old butterfly-goddess, a huge and monstrous insect-bird descending from the sky, from the gods, for vengeance—forty times the size of a vulture, magnificent in black and red.

She wants, she *dares*, someone to come along now, pin her down by the wings, and try to steal the fire from her soul. Because this time she knows what to do: She will chain him to a rock and, for the rest of eternity, pick out his eyes. Just let him come and try to fight her *now*.

6.

"Look," she says pleasantly. They are spreading a picnic out on the grass. She and her friend Suzanne are unpacking the contents of the hamper onto a tattered tablecloth: sliced meats, mustard, cheese, smoked fish, French bread, wine, and grapes. Mozart plays from someone else's radio. The statues of the two lions watch them hungrily. A squirrel scurries up a tree.

She lies down on the grass, legs sprawled open, one arm flung over her eyes. They are old friends and do not need to talk. She lies there while Suzanne lays out everything neatly: cloth napkins each containing a knife, fork and spoon (even though there is nothing they could possibly need a spoon for). Flowers in a little vase, for her birthday.

Lazily, she says to Suzanne, "You think of everything, don't you? Even spoons, that we don't even need."

"You're wrong," says Suzanne, "they're for the sherbet."

She turns over on her side, raises herself onto one elbow, and squints quizzically at her friend. Suzanne lifts up a small frozen container, like a wineglass in a toast, and explains:

"One of the customs at my father's restaurant: something tangy, something fresh, *le sorbet maison*, mango orange peach, to clear the palate, divide between the courses. To not be unfair to what follows the fish."

7

She has a massive hunger, a hunger that won't go away. It is like a stretching tiger, a yawning Moloch, that requires another, yet another, sacrifice—another infant babe to devour.

She has no name for this hunger. As a child she ate huge amounts, and ravenously. She wasn't fussy, she ate anything and everything, she ate as though striving for obesity, but she never got fat. It burned off her like Moloch's fire, she was never even full.

In adolescence, she fed on sex. She was not drawn by men, but fuelled by hunger, by clawing voraciousness. She didn't want many men, she just wanted one who could feed her, could fill her. She went through many men—the furnace billowed, *More! More! More!* The men were burnt like sacrifices.

And now, at forty, after years of madness, of hollow hunger, she has found words. There are enough of these: enough books of them, enough intensity, a single page (of Roethke, for example) can fill her for almost a day. Sometimes she is somewhere where she cannot read (in a meeting, or teaching, or making love with her husband), but she knows the books are waiting for her, they will not run away. They will be there to feed her when she gets back, when she opens her mouth to let them in. Sometimes, though, she is afraid. She is afraid they will fill her and take her over like a baby monster, like the cats the Nazis used to sew, anesthetized, inside the bellies of pregnant women. When the cats woke, they would scratch their way out, clawing to shreds the baby and the mother's insides, destroying her for having let them in.

At other times, she is fearless. And then, when some words, magic words, creep deep inside her (even four small words like *"the gray bird, sadness"*), she tears the page out of the book and eats it like a sacred ritual, chewing solemnly, and swallowing painfully around the sharp edges of paper, which slice her throat with paper cuts as

~
41

she swallows. It is an old, a primitive rite—the way men drank the blood of oxen to gain the strength of the ox: Women like her, mad women, witches, eat paper, eat pages, eat words, to stave off their hunger, they devour to keep from being devoured.

They burn like book burnings, at the same temperature as words.

8.

She has just finished a bath, and is sitting naked at her make-up table, in front of a mirror.

She looks at her reflection, and then looks away. At and away, at and away, like a girl noticing a boy, but too shy, too well-brought-up, to look right at him. She has never looked at herself, at her body, openly or closely. The idea of doing so flits across her mind; but it is so shocking, it makes her laugh out loud. She has always been shy by nature, and she was also raised to be very modest. But more than this, she is afraid. She is afraid of her body, and the pain it has known. It has been held, and wanted; but it has also been hit and wounded. And it has carried death inside its womb.

Yet her eyes are drawn upward, and she looks for herself in the glass.

In the sun-filled mirror, her eyes shine greenly back at her like a cat's, her hair is wild and mane-like; and her body, from the soft, lightly freckled shoulders down to her breasts, is perfect, perfectly formed in every way. And even the parts below that, that don't conform to current fashion—she in another time would have been a Rubens: ample, soft. There are loving, warm, admiring, luminescent paintings (she has seen them hanging in the gallery) of women with bellies and hips and thighs and buttocks exactly like hers, bathing or lolling, just as she lolls now in front of the mirror after her bath.

With surprise she sees, for the first time, that she is beautiful. Beautiful not like a face on a magazine cover, but the way that an apple tree is beautiful, or a bright-eyed pigeon in the park, or a stranger daydreaming, naked-faced, opposite you on the bus. She feels a sudden desire to be faithful, more faithful than she's ever been to any man. Faithful to this face in the mirror, to this woman: to speaking her own language from this point on, to only using words formed in her own mouth. To never lie again.

Now she sits back in her chair, and from a distance, admires the woman in the mirror: her rosy beautiful glow, and the sheen that she emanates, like life itself, like a sun-filled peach, warm and fragrant. Unembarrassed she admires her, as if admiring someone else, or a woman in a painting, nothing to do with her. As if there weren't someone looking back at her from the mirror right now, someone beautiful, someone smiling...

The woman suddenly smiles at *her*. She couldn't be more startled if a woman painted by Rubens had winked to her from inside her frame, or blown her a kiss. She is as startled as *you* would be if I were to step through this page and extend to you my hand.

She doesn't know what to do. For an instant she thinks of smashing through the mirror, reaching inside for the smiling woman and pulling her out by the neck, like rescuing her from a burning house. But then she just leans forward, and lays her cheek against the mirror's glass. Against its smooth coolness. She shuts her eyes and rests cheek to cheek against this woman, her new-found friend.

The Lesson of the Rabbi

I.

I AND THOU

"I hate bar-mitzvahs," says her father as he drives, and her mother grunts in agreement, her mouth misshapen as she puts on lipstick looking into the mirror on the flap in front of her."Did you sign the card?" he asks. She nods.

"How much did we give him?" She waits a moment, folds up her lipstick, throws it into her purse, and then answers coldly, sarcastically: "As per your instructions, $36."

"I wonder if that's enough," he broods. "Didn't they give Jeff $50 for *his* bar-mitzvah?"

~

"We've already been through this," she says impatiently. "We agreed on $36. Now leave it."

They lapse into silence. From the middle of the back seat, between the boys, Carla watches her parents' faces in the two flap mirrors hanging down. They are reflected in separate mirrors far apart.

"You okay back there?" her father calls. The boys grunt, Carla smiles into his mirror. He smiles back at her. Fondly, happily.

"Goddamit, Harriet," he says suddenly. "You're not wearing a hat. I told you to wear a hat. We're going to an Orthodox *shul*."

"Well, I couldn't find one," she answers him petulantly. She sounds like a little girl. Carla has heard this thousands of times, her petty rebellions, her refusals, her constant simmering anger always ready to flare. Furiously, her father flicks on the radio. She hears the familiar theme of a Mozart piano concerto, one of her father's favourites, and she watches the tension in his face begin to fade. Her mother is digging around in her purse and pulls out a small paperback volume of Shakespeare's sonnets. From the label on its side, Carla knows it is one of the books her mother has brought home this weekend for company, from the library where she works as Head Librarian. Her mother and father each have their own language, they each have their solitude. *Two Solitudes*, thinks Carla, the book she is in the middle of.

At the synagogue, she sits in the women's section. Her mother lifts a copy of the Pentateuch from the book rack in front of her and skims it, her thin lips pursed, her eyes narrow. A dark, burly man is mounting the steps to the podium. Her mother points to the book in the rack in front of Carla. "Read this while the rabbi's speaking," she says. "The commentaries are quite interesting." Carla takes the book and opens it to the first page. "In the beginning God created the heaven and the earth. Now the earth was

unformed and void, and darkness was upon the face of the deep..."
It reminds her of last year's grade nine English text: *The footnote
on this line refers to similar creation stories from other cultures,
for instance, Babylonian and Egyptian, and expounds on some of
the symbolic meanings of the Biblical story.* She is just beginning
to read, when suddenly she hears a loud bang, and looks up, startled, at the podium. The rabbi has pounded on the lectern, and it
sounds like something has fallen to the floor with a crash.

He is shouting.

"Do you think..." he is crying out to the assembled congregants, and pauses. *Do you think? No, most people don't,* thinks
Carla. *What a stupid question. Mind you, he's only a rabbi, what do
you expect?*

The rabbi flings his arm high in the air, and Carla is certain
that the glasses he is holding lightly in his hand will fly away. But
they don't.

"Do you think," he leans forward and croons in an intimate
and confidential voice, "that the rabbis were *stupid*?"

Carla flushes. He has caught her. He has read her mind. He
looks around the room and now he is looking at her. She looks
down.

"Do you think," he asks, his voice going higher with each
word, and ending in a pitch of passion, "that they really thought
that Adam and Eve were the only two people in the whole wide
world?"

I dunno, thinks Carla numbly. *I guess they did. Isn't that what it
says?*

"*No!*" He is screaming again. Carla feels personally screamed
at, assaulted. She feels frightened, like he is telling her she is stupid. What is he trying to say?

"Of course not!" he shouts. Then he continues quite calmly, and suddenly he is discoursing about loneliness, his own loneliness, and the need for love and comfort. He is talking tenderly, intimately, as though describing to this roomful of strangers the very inside of his soul. Carla knows he is married, she remembers vaguely that his daughter has just started at her high school, one year behind her— a big, horsey girl whom nobody likes. His wife is probably sitting here in the women's section, somewhere nearby.

"When two people love each other," he is explaining, "it is *as if* they are the only two people in the whole world. When lovers speak to each other nakedly, with the essence of their beings, when they speak to each other with Buber's 'I-Thou', then they can see nobody else, nobody else is real for them. Never mind desiring another: The world is confined, bounded, limited by the one you love."

Carla knows exactly what he means. She has just finished reading *The Little Prince* by Saint-Exupéry: "That which is essential is invisible to the eye." It is only the inner life, the felt truth, the thing that is loved, that is real. Not the apparent, the obvious, the socially confirmed.

He pounds the lectern again, and this time his glasses do go flying. The cantor, seated a few feet behind him, gets a startled, comical look on his face as they fall into his lap. He rises pompously and brings them back to the rabbi, who laughs. The rabbi has a brilliant smile, dazzling in its warmth and suddenness. Carla hasn't noticed till now how warm, how attractive, he is. She wishes now that she had dressed better, worn her pretty pink sweater and her new corduroy skirt.

"Moishe, you should play for the Dodgers," he jokes, and the congregation, carefully, politely, laughs with him. Then, just as everyone's loosening up again, his tone changes. He is suddenly menacing, angry. Immediately the congregation turns silent, serious. Almost fearful, Carla thinks.

"Make no mistake!" he is shouting. "It takes work! No one falls in love and stays in love. *The rabbis knew this!* They knew this! You don't believe me? You think they were any different from you? *No! They struggled!* They also wondered sometimes..." Here he laughs charmingly, as if mocking himself. But then his voice rises again. "But this is the power of moral thinking—this is the power of a vision based not on beauty, but on meaning; not on art (the Nazis loved their music and their literature), but on spirituality; not on passion, but on love." His voice rises in intensity and ends in a passionate falsetto climax: "This is the meaning of a life not of love affairs with men or women, but of a love affair with God." He looks drained, he pauses and breathes deeply. "A love affair with God," he says quietly, then "*Shabbat Shalom*," and steps back to his seat near the cantor, where he slumps, exhausted, looking into his lap.

⊶⇒◉⇐⊷

Carla leaves her aunts and her parents who have clustered into little knots around the *kiddish* table. She feels strangely excited by the rabbi's talk and thinks that the story of Adam and Eve might be interesting, if read with commentaries, with a poetic sensibility, with a desire to uncover its layers. The president of the *shul* rose at the end of the service and presented her cousin Stanley with a Pentateuch, shook his hand and wished him a hearty *mazel tov*, and then went on to make announcements. One of these was about a Sunday morning class for high school students, studying with the rabbi. *It's not for me*, Carla had decided, watching the rabbi, distant and dreaming on his throne. But he piqued her interest, reminding her of Lillian, a Catholic girl she had met over the summer, who would rapturously go on and on about God and her love of God, while falling about her in droves were guys with their hands on their hearts professing love, ready to die for her. Lillian couldn't see it until Carla told her. She blushed but basically ignored this information. "It's God I love," she had said piously, and somehow Carla loved her for it, loved her for her freedom from men, for not playing the game, for not revolving around the trappings and sticky longings of teenage love and sex.

Carla wanders off by herself, to be alone, to think. She finds something lonely in these Jewish social events. They are supposed to be about community, but she has no community, she is alone, and no amount of talking, or Yiddish jokes, not even the warmth and comfort of her aunts, who always touch her—on the arm, on the hand, on the hair—can ease this constant ache. She is looking down at the ground as she walks, thinking of the rabbi's glasses flying through the air, and Adam and Eve naked in the garden, when she nearly crashes into the rabbi and his daughter coming up the stairs, arm in arm. Dina drops her father's arm and runs up to Carla. "I thought I saw you!" she cries. "What are you doing here?"

Carla feels the rabbi's eyes on her, and she is happy to be thus greeted, made important, by the daughter. "I'm here for the bar-mitzvah," she answers calmly, feeling very sophisticated next to Dina. "Stanley's my cousin."

"No kidding!" says Dina, as though it were the strangest thing on earth. She turns to her father, who is watching her fondly, with interest. "*Abba*," she says, "this is Carla, from my new school. She's a grade ahead of me, and she's really popular. Carla, this is my father."

Carla feels flattered and very strong. The rabbi shifts his gaze to her. He looks different up close, just like anybody else in a blue suit and tie, a friendly and pleasant smile. Until he looks at her. His eyes are a very deep dark brown, bordering on black, and it is with a grave intensity that he bends down and peers into her eyes (light green with specks in them), as if peering into her soul. She has learned from Lillian to look right up at other people, to be bold and brave, and not to show her shyness. She dares her eyes right up into his; but he meets and holds them, and she lowers hers first.

"I noticed you while I was speaking," he says.

"Me, too," mumbles Carla, still looking down.

Dina is watching closely. "So are you planning to come here again?" she asks, hungry for friendship.

"What for?" Carla is flustered and a little shaken by the rabbi's piercing look. "Oh, you mean the high school classes. Are you giving those?" she asks, turning back to the rabbi. He smiles a little and nods.

"Come," he says. "It'll be fun to have you. It's going to be a great class." Something in what he says angers Carla, but she's not sure what. Is it his arrogance, his assumption that he is worth listening to? Is it the way he forced her to look down? She dares her eyes upwards again, pretending she's Lillian, and opens them wide into his.

"Can you teach me about God?" she asks with mock innocence, but at the same time bluntly, as if asking a casual question, as if asking, Can he repair a sink? Does he know how to drive? She goes on, brutally, refusing to back down, "Can you teach me how to have a love affair with God?"

He stares at her for a moment, shocked. She thinks maybe she has said something really terrible. Maybe she has blasphemed (a concept she never usually thinks of at all). For a moment, as he looks at her with that expression, she is genuinely frightened. Then, suddenly, as if he has decided to, he breaks into a laugh, a warm, full laugh, with his head thrown back and his eyes shut, while she watches him uncertainly.

"A Ulysses girl," he says, referring to her high school, with its reputation for radical '60's education and prodigious, mouthy kids. He leans down, bringing his face so close to hers that she can feel his warm breath as he speaks. "Come to my class," he whispers, his eyes boring into hers. "I'll teach you what you want to know, I'll teach you how to fall in love with God."

From the corner of her eye, Carla catches Dina's worried face, looking on. "Come on, *Abba*," she's saying, pulling on her father's arm. The rabbi straightens up very slowly, and once erect, inclines his head ever so slightly towards Carla in a mock bow, the way one might honour a formidable adversary. Then he takes his daughter's arm, and the two of them, king and princess, continue majestically on their way.

⊷⊷⊷◉⊷⊷⊷

On the drive home, Carla's mother is slumped against the front door, sleeping, and in the back seat, on either side of her, Carla's brothers stare blankly out their windows. Carla surreptitiously watches her father as he drives; and although he is in expert control of the wheel, he too is absent—vacuous as he listens to Rachmaninoff. It is the Concerto #3, Carla's favourite, but she knows her father thinks it "immature." Anyway, he'd far prefer Brahms, but "what can you do?" he has told her, regretfully, on several occasions. "You can't control what's on the air."

It was always her and her father, she thinks, not necessarily against anybody, not necessarily against her mother; but they were the prime unit of the family, and even casual visitors could feel it, as Carla welcomed them, and served them tea and cakes, and sat near her father, looking up at him when he spoke. Carla got her position mainly through default, through her mother's indifference and her father's loneliness, and through looking like his dead mother, Russian and beautiful with long dark hair. Sometimes he would stand before Carla and push her long hair back behind her ears, and hold it there, staring at her, seeing his mother. He even suggested some years back that she wear it in a bun, to which Carla's mother firmly objected—and Carla was glad, aligned if only secretly with her mother just this once. She was only seven and didn't want to look like a grandmother.

Just last year, when she was fourteen, she sprouted little breasts. She thought of them as bizarre growths that were supposed to carry such meaning, they were supposed to mean she was a woman, but they didn't mean anything at all, except that now she had to wear a bra, which felt like a harness, and made her think she was now going to be somebody's horse. The other bad thing about "developing" was that her father began to change. All she had ever had was him: She would run to him when he came home from work, usually well after supper was eaten and cleaned up, and it was almost time for bed. She threw her arms around him, he laughed and swung her around, he called her "little queen" and stroked her hair, and then they went into the kitchen and she kept him company while he ate, silently serving him what she knew he liked best (black bread, cheese, tomatoes, and onions), smiling as she watched him eat. They would comfort each other in this way, without words.

But now something has changed. It is subtle, but palpable. When he comes home now, and she throws herself at him, he gets embarrassed, and pushes her away, and says things like, "My, you're getting to be a big girl." Now she no longer runs up to him, but waits in the kitchen, reading, and calls, "Hi, Dad!" She still serves him when he comes in, but some of the time now, she feels lonely and sad, or angry at him: it seems to her that he has become cruel to her. There is no way to get back to him, there is no way to get back on track.

⊷═◉═⊷

The first class with the rabbi. It is October, and they are doing *I and Thou*. She has never read this book, but she remembers the rabbi mentioning it during his sermon. She is surprised when she looks down at his copy of it that the author is not "Buba," as he pronounced it, but Buber. Martin Buber. On the cover, he has a long bearded rabbi's face—a face that interests her, in spite of herself, with its depth and sadness. *A Heart of Darkness*, she thinks.

The rabbi sits at the table, takes off his glasses, lays them gently down. He looks around at his students. There are seven of them, they are all fifteen or sixteen, and he seems suddenly sad and overwhelmed.

"You're so young," he says, "but I think you are ready for this." He seems a little afraid to begin, as though he is about to give them a great gift, and they might not like it, or they might not understand it, and will ask, holding up the present they've unwrapped: "What's *this*?" Carla feels protective of him and also has a great desire to let him know she understands, that his confidence in her is justified.

The rabbi stands up and slowly, tenderly, reads the first section. His voice is deep and resonant. He obviously loves these words, or something that is behind them, and reads them like they're poetry.

"'To Man, the world is twofold, in accordance with his twofold attitude.'"

To human beings, Carla translates to herself, *the world is twofold...*

"'The attitude of Man,'" the rabbi continues, "'is twofold, in accordance with the twofold nature of the primary words with which he speaks. The primary words are not isolated words, but combined words. The one primary word is the combination *I-Thou*. The other primary word is the combination *I-It*; wherein, without a change in the primary word, one of the words *he* and *she* can replace *it*. Hence the *I* of Man is also twofold. For the *I* of the primary word *I-Thou* is a different *I* from that of the primary word *I-It*.'"

The rabbi stops, puts down his book, and waits. The silence is dramatic. All the students look up at him, and he looks at them, probingly, one at a time.

"Now what is this?" he asks. "What's this all about?"

There is silence in the room. Carla looks around at her class-mates, none of whom she has ever seen before. They are all boys, she is the only girl, and they all look nervous, some of them are looking down. She realizes that most of them probably come to this synagogue, this is their rabbi, they have probably even been in classes with him before, and that only she is an outsider, a new-comer to this world.

But she is not afraid. She feels happy, free, she is a "free school" girl, a Ulysses girl, unintimidated by "the great rabbi." This is not a world she has to take seriously. This is just a provin-cial sub-world, the religious Jewish community, it is something she can play with. Anyway, she's always gotten A's in English, and she thinks she understands perfectly what this passage is about. She can feel the depth and power of this book. This is the kind of book she has been waiting for.

The silence builds, and the rabbi is getting impatient: He is pacing back and forth in front of them as though the room is too small.

A skinny boy on Carla's left ventures an answer: "Maybe it's about faith in God."

The rabbi listens, staring intensely straight ahead as he con-tinues to prowl. Without looking at the boy, he answers him in a tone that is driving, almost bullying:

"What about it, Irwin? What about faith in God?" His voice is rising in intensity, the silence grows; and fierce with frustration, he roars at them, "Come on! Come on! It's not such a hard ques-tion! What do you think this is about?"

Carla does not know that this is how he teaches. She thinks he is angry at all of them, including her, and she begins to feel a little panicky, the way she felt as a little girl when her mother's voice began to rise, when the anger began to escalate, and she realized, with a sinking heart, that there was no way she could alter its course, either divert or reverse it, and prevent the explosion. They are three minutes into the class, fifty-seven left to go, and she finds the tension unbearable. Furthermore, the answer seems obvious to her, and she doesn't understand why all the boys are looking down. She speaks up softly.

"It's about reality, isn't it?" The rabbi stops pacing and looks at her. He leans forward to catch her voice which has gone a little breathless. "On the one hand, there are the everyday things, you do the everyday things of life: you buy things, you use things. And then there's really seeing The Other. Something or someone...in their fullness, in their *reality*. I think Buber's talking about that whole other dimension, that way of relating."

He stares at her while she speaks, and when she's finished, he is still staring, speechless. Then he catches himself, and turns to include the rest of the class.

"Exactly!" he says; but he is not bombastic any more, and as he expounds on this idea and develops it and plays with it and challenges it, his eyes keep wandering back to Carla, as if he is puzzling her out: *Who is she? How did she know that?* Carla feels it, too, feels her power, her position in the class, for having given just the right answer, for having pleased him. She is aware of the boys noticing her, too, partly with admiration, partly with resentment.

The next class and all the ones that follow are like the first: as sharp and shining as the edge of a knife, with the ever-present glint of danger. The rabbi teaches with passion that gradually mounts throughout the hour. Sometimes when he is so moved that he cannot, standing still, contain the lyricism in an idea or a text, he lifts his arms and dances. He ends each class whispering, as though the climax of their study together is the most private of secrets: "To speak with one's essence the *I* of *I-Thou* is to enter into a dialogical existence, into a different relationship with the world—one of intense, almost unbearable, intimacy, a relationship of profound but tragic passion." Then there is a single business-like sentence ("For next time read section four") and he is gone, leaving his young students sitting there, electrified and a little dazed for a few seconds, before rustling together their papers and silently shuffling out.

⊷━◉━⊶

Over the weeks, the rabbi enters her through her mind—the only place there is to enter her, being who she is—which means that he also has possession of her soul. Her mind is the tunnel to her very essence, the way in some old houses, dark living rooms give out onto bay windows overlooking the lawn, and sun porches drenched with light. She believes, like her mother, in books, and thinks that through books, and only through books, can she solve the problem of evil and pain in the world and the riddle of her own life—her mother's violent hatred of her and her own terrible loneliness. She has read a tremendous amount for her age, but there is still a book she has been waiting for, a book like *I and Thou*, which will teach her another language: the language of love, the language of her soul. In the desperateness of her waiting, she has seemed to those around her as strange and as touched as Hamlet, whom they are studying in school. Her teachers decide she is "going through something," maybe she is in love. One day, in art class, imitating pointillism, she takes a flat-topped glue brush and in an hour creates a portrait of darkness that brings the school psychologist running. Carla feels nothing but contempt. "Of course it's dark: life is dark. Anyway, there's a little yellow in the corner, so calm down."

In November, at the fourth class, the rabbi asks how many of them have read Heschel, and when the boys look down and Carla is silent, he throws his book down on the table, and bellows, "What the hell do you do with your time? What have you people been doing for the past fifteen years?" At the end of class, Carla goes up to him as he is leaving and tells him what she has read over the past year, and he sneers at her before walking away: "Oh, I see. You read only Christians. It's easier, isn't it, to love others than your own."

She stands there shocked, horrified at what he has said. She has never thought of Shakespeare as Christian, though she supposes he was. Is the rabbi saying that Shakespeare (and Steinbeck and Sartre) aren't worth reading because they aren't Jewish? Is he discounting, discarding everyone and everything else in the world but Jewish philosophers and poets? She feels furious, and faintly nauseated, at his implication. Yet gradually, over the next few weeks, she also begins to see his point. Why *had* she never read the prophets, or the Yiddish classics, or modern Hebrew poetry? They all exist in translation; they just have never existed for her. For the first time, Carla questions her views, which are her father's views. In her mind, the rabbi argues with her father, exposing the shallowness of her father's liberal humanism, the naiveté of his universalism, the lack of firm core, absolute principle, in his philosophy. She begins to see her father as wishy-washy and sentimental, hiding behind beautiful music, and not facing facts. Also for the first time, she takes advantage of her school's policy of optional classes, and starts skipping biology, geography, and history every afternoon, in order to read in the library at the synagogue.

She reads there almost every day, from after lunch until it closes. She reads voraciously, book after book, on Creation, the Flood, the Binding of Isaac, and God's place in history. But most desperately, most hungrily, she reads about Man and God, and the possibilities between them. She reads Heschel's trilogy, linked like Abraham, Isaac and Jacob: *Man Is Not Alone*, *Man's Quest for God*, and (with delight) *God In Search of Man*. She encounters Soloveitchik's essay, "The Lonely Man of Faith," and suddenly realizes that among all these other lonely, yearning souls, she is no longer lonely. When she reads here in this library, she hears the rabbi's voice. In a way he is there, reading with her, reading to her; and when she disagrees with something, she fights with the author as he would fight, she and he fighting together, on the same team, against Erich Fromm or Mordecai Kaplan. "Are you saying," she says to Fromm, her inner voice taking on a trace of the rabbi's Brooklyn accent, and also his contempt, "that a Man can become a God? How can you say such a thing?!"

She reads Heschel's *The Earth is the Lord's* and *The Sabbath*, and she weeps.

⊷⊶⊙⊶⊷

It is early December, when it is already dark by 4:30, and Carla has been invited for Friday night supper at the rabbi's. She arrives early, a good half-hour before sundown, as Dina has told her to, and she meets Ricky, the rabbi's wife, for the first time. Somehow she assumed that Ricky would look either plain and beige like a rabbi's wife, or big and broad-shouldered and vulgar with too much make-up, like Dina. But Ricky has a perfect body, and is very sexy in a straight grey skirt, a close-fitting cashmere sweater, and stockinged feet. She has wide sea-blue eyes, a glowing complexion, and a smile that is ravishing but mischievous, inviting friendship. Carla is dazzled.

Ricky does not seem to her like a rabbi's wife at all: She seems perfectly normal, like someone she could be friends with. Unlike Dina, she is open and accessible, and Carla learns within the first twenty minutes that Ricky wasn't brought up religious, she was working as a model when she first met her husband. Now she likes to invent strange and slightly bizarre clothes for herself (felt slippers, for instance, like Peter Pan's) out of the kids' arts and crafts materials and various old clothes. Then Ricky says, "Excuse me," and with a charming smile, lies down flat on the floor and looks up at Carla. "I like to see things sometimes," she says, "from a different angle. Know what I mean?" and gives her a wink. Carla is too shy to join her on the floor, but stares at her, hypnotized, as Ricky directs and organizes the whole household from her position on the floor, telling the children what to wear, mediating their arguments, warning them to turn off the iron they used for their last-minute, pre-*Shabbat* pressings. Carla is smitten by this wonderful happy child-woman, someone it is hard to think of as anybody's mother. When Dina comes over to say she can smell the chicken burning, Ricky giggles and winks at Carla like a conspirator, and stays prone on the floor. She is having fun, she waves to the rabbi like a little girl when he walks in. He just grins when he sees her. Then he waves and says "Welcome" to Carla, and runs up the stairs, two at a time, to change.

Now that the sun has set, everyone is sitting, freshly scrubbed and dressed, around the table laid with a white linen cloth, and to Carla it seems that the rabbi and his wife are completely filled with light. They are calm and radiant, and after the blessings over the wine and the braided *challah*, the rabbi then blesses each of his children, as though each one is a personal vineyard or wheatfield. He places both his hands on the bowed clean heads (Sarah's with her curly hair is a grapevine; Samuel's and Dina's, straight-haired, are fields of tired wheat), his lips moving as he mutters blessings over them, and then ends with a soft kiss on each forehead. Carla stands awkwardly before him, and uncertainly, he blesses her, too. Carla notices that only he does the blessing, no one blesses him, because—she supposes—he is so strong, he doesn't need one. She wonders where the word "bless" comes from; in French, which she is learning at school, "blesser" means to hurt. Ricky waits on him with food, with platters of vegetables, and chicken, and potatoes, and afterwards she serves him honey cake and tea.

Carla knew that at her house, her parents would be eating alone, the boys out playing hockey or at friends' houses, and she over here with the rabbi's family. Maybe her parents would have defrosted a little turd of meatloaf, and because it was heated up on the highest possible heat (because her father was so hungry and her mother hadn't prepared for him ahead of time), the out-side would be charred and the inside a cold, frozen lump, with varying degrees of warmth or coolness waving unpredictably through every bite.

Or possibly, her father would be eating alone. He would be in his bathrobe, his naked feet up on the empty chair opposite, read-ing the paper while he nibbled at some bread and cheese. He would pretend he didn't care; but later on he'd find an excuse to criticize her mother and pick a fight, and the evening would end in shouts and recriminations. Or just as often, in silence: those old wooden doors shutting carefully, finally, against each other, and her mother sleeping on the cot in the den.

Here it is all light. Everybody is singing songs that Carla doesn't understand, but she hums along anyway, they seem sweet and faintly familiar, as though she's heard them somewhere before, though she is sure she hasn't. The rabbi and his wife sit at the head and the foot of the table, and look at each other with pleasure across the long length of it. Carla knows, from something Irwin has said in class, that on *Shabbat* one gets an extra soul from heaven, and therefore it is a special *mitzvah* to make love on Friday night. She can feel the two of them waiting, the stretch of the elastic between them, as they wait for their time, the night.

After dinner, there is more singing: *Shabbos* songs about God, about holiness, about the joys of the Sabbath, and after the singing, more talk, and after the talk, the cake and fruit, and then more singing, and then a loud and rowdy prayer-song, the blessing after the meal, thanking God for the food, and the company, and the beauty of the holy Sabbath. By the end of the meal, Carla has fallen in love: with *Shabbat*, with holiness, with this happy, singing family. That night, when everyone has gone to bed, and the house is quiet and full of peace, she lies awake in the bed they have made up for her in the basement (because on *Shabbat* you don't drive or travel—you leave technology behind, and return to the time of creation—and her parents' house is too far away to walk to). She lies on her back with her hands clasped behind her neck, wondering why she has wasted so much time. Staring at the ceiling, she thinks, *Now I'm at home. My real life is starting now.*

·──◉━◉──·

That night, she dreams she is standing in a street downtown, looking into the window of a jewelry store. All by itself, on its own velvet cushion, is a jade statue in the shape of a Buddha. Enigmatically smiling, the rotund figure is smooth and rich-green and, although Carla usually doesn't take to this sort of thing, quite compelling. He has the round peacefulness of her father's face, the same apparently simple but impenetrable smile and the arrogance of his confident, classic pose. As she gazes at it, thinking that Buddha is eternal—that he will live forever, if only you believe—her father begins to melt. He has turned into one of those candles you buy in cheap stores reeking of incense, and even though he has no wick, he is melting slowly, starting with a small but widening pool at the top of his head, as soft green as the pool in the glade in *A Midsummer Night's Dream*. As she watches, horrified, unable to break through the glass, the Buddha is slowly melting, smiling unbearably mildly, *just the way Daddy would*, she thinks approvingly, right in the middle of her dream—*mildly, gently, in classical form*. Now the head is gone, now the shoulders, now the top of his torso, down, down, past the knees, to a little waxy pool at his feet, and her father is gone. She watches helplessly from behind the glass. She watches, loving him, and loving the melted jade.

⊷═◉═⊷

Two days later, at the last class of the term, they wrap up *I and Thou*, which, Carla presumes, is the basis for redemption, because next term, starting in January (while at school they will be learning in physics about the heat of vaporization, in geography about deserts, and in history about World War I and the Depression), here they are going to do Redemption. The rabbi has mentioned Franz Rosenzweig's *The Star of Redemption* in his last few classes. He has said several times, "Now I can't go into this now, but you'll see, next term, when we study this, it'll all fall into place. Then you'll *really* understand Buber." Carla feels she is being teased, like when she was a child and couldn't understand a joke and was told she would when she was "older." She feels she is older now, but apparently she is still not quite ready for the real, the big, secret. But next term she will be, and she will learn it then.

As she follows the others out of the class, and then rides home on the bus, she is teeming with the ideas the rabbi has filled her with. Before she met him, the Ulysses School had emptied her of hope, of meaning, by teaching her carefully, deliberately, systematically the contrast between the highest ideals and the workings of this world. *Richard III* terrified her; *The Red Badge of Courage* and *Black Like Me* made her—like the best of her classmates (many of whom turned to drugs)—bitter and cynical. Her school shook her faith in the world, and her family cracked her heart. But she is not yet broken. Somehow the rabbi has penetrated the fortress of her cynicism and disillusion, and his ideas have filled her with hope. What she once scorned as provincial sentimentality, as irrational opiate, and as ghetto-like in its narrowness, she now understands as not only congruent with reason, but as a coherent and complete language for her spiritual-intellectual life. Heschel responded to, argued with, and ultimately triumphed over Kierkegaard on existential angst and loneliness; Fackenheim won the debate with Hegel on history; and the *Torah* wiped out both Blake and Christian theology, the stuff of Lillian's letters, with a firm, swift hand. Carla still struggles with the idea of God, the God whose name is so holy you are not allowed to speak it except in prayer; in everyday speech, He is nameless, referred to only as "The Name" or "Holy One, Blessed Be He." She still hasn't dared to ask the rabbi about that old man sitting on a cloud, pulling strings, like George Bernard Shaw on the cover of her "My Fair Lady" record. She also doesn't see any place for women in Judaism; and she can't really believe that God intervenes in history, that God actually cares about human comings and goings, or more particularly about hers...But there seems in this Jewish way of life a better, a happier, way to live. "Is the happy life the good life?" the rabbi once asked, half-joking, in class. "Absolutely," she answered, without hesitation. For instance, when she thinks about him and his wife looking down the long table at each other, when she sees the jubilation in his teaching and the way he takes steps two at a time—there is meaning, or the possibility of it; there is a little bit of hope.

II.

REDEMPTION

Carla spends the Christmas vacation with her family. They fly down to Florida and stay with her grandmother, who is depressed and complains and carps at her mother. Her mother, in turn, criticizes Carla ceaselessly on everything from her posture to her grammar. While the boys play ping-pong and swim, and her father reads in the sun, Carla's headaches come back, the ones that miraculously all but disappeared during the fall term.

They drive home from the airport, and as soon as they enter the house, Carla heads straight to her room, puts on Beethoven's nine symphonies, takes out her copy of *I and Thou*, and doesn't resurface until the next morning when she has to go back to school. She thinks of nothing but the rabbi and his promises about Redemption. The idea of redemption is strange to her, she has never thought about it before; and in her parents' old house, stinking with anger and hate, she cannot believe, except with a corner of her mind—the yellow corner of memory—that anything like it is possible.

But at his first class in January, it happens all over again. She is inspired by Rosenzweig's story: a man confined to a wheelchair, whose sum total of movement, of physical capacity, is to blink his eyes; and who singlehandedly built a brilliant and influential institute of Jewish learning, the *lehrhaus*, in post–World War I Frankfurt. Like Carla, he was from an irreligious background, both secular and cynical, and lived in a place and time as sophisticated, as alienated, as lost, as her own. But with the blink of his eyes, he opened those of his assimilated Jewish friends and acquaintances, introducing them to God and to the possibility of redemption, thus drawing them into the limelight, the centre, of history from their place on the periphery. Carla has both her eyes; she also has a strong, healthy body, two arms, two legs. It emboldens her, fires her, to think what she could do and accomplish—if she had the will. And she is finding the will, she is finding a language for her soul and her life.

At the end of this class, the other students file out, but Carla is still writing in her notebook. The rabbi watches her from his seat.

"How was your holiday?" he asks.

She looks up. "Okay," she says. "It was Christmas."

He laughs appreciatively. Then he muses, "You seem so much to want to learn. I have never in my life met anyone with such a passion for learning."

"I know," she says eagerly, "but I don't know why. I think, anyway, I must be crazy, seeking knowledge like this, wanting to learn everything. Because the more I learn, the sadder I get. That's the main thing I've found out so far."

"How do you know that?" he asks her urgently, almost angrily. "Did you read that somewhere?" She shakes her head. "That's from *Koheles*, from Ecclesiastes. How can you know that at your age? How old are you, anyway?"

"Fifteen," she says. "I don't know how I know, I just do. I've always thought about stuff like this."

"You are so wise for your age," he says, as if to himself. "It is almost frightening."

Carla grins and shrugs. She suddenly feels older than this

rabbi, he seems so naive, so easily impressed and shocked, knowing nothing about things, like drugs, that she lives with every day.

"No, I'm not," she says cheerfully. She is happy that he likes her, that she has dazzled him back a little bit. "I'm just regular."

He is staring at her.

"Who are you?" he asks. "What does your father do?"

Carla hesitates. She always answers this question carefully. "He's a public servant," she says. And then, "Not really, that's just our answer we joke about at home. He's in Trudeau's cabinet."

The rabbi's eyes widen. "Tobin, of course," is all he says, "I've seen him in the papers." But she feels how impressed he is and, for the first time, he has disappointed her. She feels contempt for him.

Then he asks, casually, "Your parents—are they happy together? Do they love each other?"

She is shocked by his question, the bluntness of it; but she steels herself, much as she steels herself when she undresses in front of the doctor ("He's a doctor after all," she always tells herself). She pauses. On the one hand, fifteen years of family loyalty, deeply ingrained, struggle within her; on the other, she wants to tell the truth, she was taught as a child not to lie, and she wants to tell it to *him*. She looks up at him, and there is nothing sinister on his face.

"No," she says, looking directly at him, "they are not happy. My parents fight a lot, and I get stuck in the middle." She pauses again, full of fear, but he doesn't say anything, and she feels impelled to continue. "If I make supper, I'm trying to take her place; if I don't, I'm a crappy daughter, why don't I ever help? Whatever I do is wrong. Sometimes I think I'll go crazy. I hate it. I hate that house."

She has never told anyone this before, and she is inwardly trembling. She thinks that the heavens will cave in, she will be struck down for breaking faith, for breaking the image. But she goes on. She tells him what she has managed to keep from the school psychologist, from the family doctor who she thinks has suspected for years, from the world at large, to protect her father.

"She hates me," she whispers to him. "She really *hates* me. Sometimes she's really crazy."

She stops, terrified. Somehow speaking has made it real. She stares at the rabbi.

"And your father?" he asks. "What about your father?"

She continues to stare, not understanding the question.

He explains quite patiently, not the way he teaches; but there is still something relentless in it, something brutal. "Why doesn't he help you? Why doesn't he *do* something?"

Still, she stares at him, uncomprehending. It has never entered her mind that her father should, or could, do anything, or that she should expect him to. And also, there is an edge to the rabbi's voice when he talks about her father that she can't quite name, but she feels it is there, and it silences her. They go on to talk of other things; but she is exhausted, and when she gets up to leave, she feels raw, and drained, and confused.

He asks Carla, as they stand by the door, to keep on being Dina's friend, to come over as often as she wants (she is welcome any time), that he would personally appreciate it, he worries about his daughter. He tells Carla that she is a very special person, that she has a brilliant mind and a beautiful soul, and that he is honoured to be her teacher. She has a sudden impulse to hug him, the way she would hug her father; and then she remembers that Orthodox men, not to mention rabbis, do not touch women, except their wives, and even then under very strict and controlled circumstances. So she just turns away, and wanders toward the door of the synagogue, blushing and a little dazed. Only through a haze, as she leaves, does she hear the rabbi pointing her out to someone as "Tobin's daughter"; but this, which would normally revolt her, doesn't bother her at all. Along with her flushing euphoria, she feels shame, as though she's been stripped, and hasn't had time enough to dress, as though she has been triumphed over. She is still confused and shaken an hour later, after the long bus ride home.

⊶═◉═⊷

After this, Carla begins dropping by his house more, without invitation, and she is always made to feel welcome. The door is never locked, they never ask her why she's come or how long she's staying, and the bed in the basement is always made up. After a few weeks, her arrival no longer prompts anyone to stand up and come over to greet her at the door. They stay where they are, continue what they're doing, and just wave, or smile. Carla makes herself at home, usually goes down to the basement first and puts away her clothes and books. Then if she's hungry, she goes to the fridge and helps herself. Once in a while she offers food to others. Most often she just sprawls out on the couch and reads.

Because it is winter and *Shabbat* comes in so early, on Fridays the synagogue library shuts at one, so she just goes to the rabbi's house straight from school. And on Saturday night, there doesn't seem much point in going home just to sleep, when she has her Sunday class the next morning at ten. And after the class, she comes back to their house for lunch, or stays to study at the library and then drops over in mid-afternoon.

So it ends up that she is spending pretty much all weekend, every weekend, with the rabbi and his family. There are also a lot of weeknight events at the synagogue which she attends and then sleeps over: a concert in Jewish soul music with Shlomo Carlebach, "the singing rabbi," or a lecture by a visiting scholar, which the rabbi subsequently rips to shreds. And of course, every Wednesday night there is the rabbi's study group on the weekly Bible portion, which Carla sometimes goes to with Dina, walking there and back in the cold winter darkness with her hands in her pockets. In this way, the winter term speeds by, even though not much of anything actually happens, in much the same way that on holidays, once a routine is established, the time just seems to devour itself.

Once, a couple of weeks after their conversation, Carla asked the rabbi if they could talk again sometime. He seemed a little confused, almost as if he'd forgotten their discussion. "Oh, yeah, sure," he said; but he never brought it up again, and she was too embarrassed and proud to ask a second time.

But still she talks to him, anyway. He has become so much a part of her, that anything she thinks or feels that is beautiful or profound she attributes to him. She is certain that before she met him, she had never seen anything, she had never felt anything, she had never known beauty. On the bus to *shul*, gazing out the window at the back, she tells him about everything she passes, as though unless she tells it to him, it is not real. She tells him about the exquisite patterns made by the rain on the back window, shot through like diamonds with light, merging, separating, and swirling infinitely, unpredictably, like the holy sparks that together would one day unite and save the world. She also tells him things about herself, long, intricate stories; and by the time she gets to *shul*, she is exhausted from telling him everything, from explaining to him, picturing him, smiling at him, confiding in him. And by the time she sees him, there is nothing left to say; she has already told him everything. Why go over it again?

In class, she stumbles. She doesn't seem to catch his points as adroitly as before. Sometimes she gives the right answer, but more often, when he turns to her, she looks at him blankly, almost frightened, as though she's been away, somewhere else, not even listening. The rabbi stops looking only to her for understanding. More often now he is pleased by Irwin, or one of the others.

At school, she has skipped her classes all term, even the mornings, and when she sits to write her exams, she can't even make educated guesses. She writes brief and foolish answers, knowing they are wrong, knowing as she writes that she has failed yet another exam.

What were the causes of the First World War?
Lack of higher purpose. Lack of hope. Insufficient love.

⤖⚬⚬⤛

In June, now that school's out, Carla has no reason to go home at all, and she stays at the rabbi's, one-more-night, one-more-night, for almost three weeks. When she calls home one more time to say she'll be staying over, her father tells her he'd like to see her face once in a while so he can remember what she looks like. She hangs up, tells Ricky and the rabbi she'll see them on *Shabbat*, and heads for home.

A few hours later, she is back. The rabbi is alone in the kitchen, leaning back against the counter on one elbow, munching on some *challah*. He straightens up, surprised, when he sees her.

"Hi," he says.

She stands very still in the doorway, not answering.

He squints at her. "What's the matter?" he asks. "You look like Elijah after a vision."

She shrugs and looks down, and starts to cry—so quietly that it takes him a few moments to understand from the convulsing of her shoulders. He comes over and bends his head down, trying to look into her eyes.

"What is it, Carla? What's happened?"

She shakes her head from side to side, refusing speech like a child. Then she turns her face away, and now the marks on her neck show: long red scratches and finger gouges and a sprawling yellow bruise. The rabbi's breath sucks in sharply and he pulls back from her, standing straight up. From his full height, he looks down and sees the top of her head and the blood caking black in her hair. His face twists as if he will vomit, his eyes shut tight.

"My God," he says.

There is the sound of her quiet sobbing.

"Can I stay here?" she asks, looking up at him. "Don't tell me to go. I can't go home, don't make me go home."

The rabbi stands there dazed. She watches his white shock colour into anger, it rises and trembles in him when he says, "That crazy woman, I'll kill her." Then he looks down at Carla, and his voice is gentle when he speaks. "Of course you can stay here. As long as you want."

She steps forward, closing the one step between them, and leans her weight against him. She can feel his surprise. He doesn't hold her but he also doesn't push her away. She lays her head into the hollow of his arm, presses it as if sticking her head inside a cave, into an opening like a vagina, as though she would push her head through and bury herself inside him. She can feel his shock at the contact with her body. Then she feels his hand, wondering, on her hair.

→══◉══←

The usual routine continues, the change is minimal, except that now Dina is in Israel for the summer, so Carla has taken over her room. She doesn't think about going home any more. She can't even picture sleeping in her own bed again without feeling the beginning of one of her headaches, so all month she has refused to think about it at all.

The rabbi and his wife have not asked her to explain anything. They treat her just as they have all year, but even more tenderly, like a child. They cut everything—chicken, bread, watermelon—into five equal parts, one for her, as though she has always been a part of their family. She is soothed, or at least numbed, being near them.

But at night, every few nights, she has nightmares. On the first night, she awakens to find the rabbi standing over her, staring down at her. She is startled and raises herself on her elbows.

"You were screaming," he says. "Are you okay?"

She nods, shocked in that half-place between sleep and waking, the cold darkness she has wakened into more like sleep than like life. She is shivering, her nightgown is drenched, and rising up from it is a sour smell, like rotting grapes.

"What did I say?" she asks.

His face is in shadow, he is a stone-grey archway over her, a rainbow over flat land when the light from the window haloes his hair into gold. His bathrobe is loosely tied, she obviously roused him. He sighs. "Nothing," he says. "You were just screaming."

His shadow moves over to the Venetian blinds. She thinks maybe she is still dreaming, as she lies back under the thin blanket in the white cotton nightgown Ricky has lent her, watching him curiously, almost dispassionately, thinking, as if watching a movie, *He is going to kiss me.* He is facing out the window and fingering the blinds thoughtfully, like reading Braille. He strokes them slowly, back and forth, one at a time, and then stops and turns around to face her. He comes over toward the bed and looks down at her directly, a look almost hard on his face. "Are you okay?" he asks her, and his voice is hoarse and low; it is a voice she has not heard before. She nods, looking up into his eyes, those intense brown eyes that seem to bore into her, through the blanket, through the sheet, through the nightgown. He continues to stare at her heavily, and then finally nods, with a philosophical smile that turns up only one side of his mouth. "Sleep," he says, and is gone, like Hamlet's father, an apparition.

⤛══○══⤜

These are her nights. Every few nights she wakes screaming after dreaming and the rabbi comes in to her room. But in the daytime, she is her usual self. She goes to the last class on Redemption, a special, full-day class. Instead of the usual last-class review and summary, the rabbi has chosen to set his students a challenge. They are each to find one question (never mind the answer, this is unimportant), and they have until 4:00 to search for it. There is excitement in the class, the tone of a scavenger hunt; and they work hard all day searching in *chevrusa*, in study pairs. Now it is 4:00 and they are presenting their questions, gifts to each other, gifts to the rabbi. Most of them are biographical, about Rosenzweig and his experience of redemption. Irwin's is finely philosophical, involving definitions and redefinitions of Redemption: *pilpul*, the art of splitting hairs. The rabbi takes Carla's question last.

"613 commandments!" she says bluntly, referring to the path to redemption the rabbi has taught them, Maimonides' guide to the moral life. "It's too many. Who could possibly do them all? Who can even remember them?"

The rabbi laughs briefly and nods. Then he looks grave. "I know," he says. "It's hard to be good." He sits at the table with them, takes off his glasses, and rubs his eyes with an expression of pain. Then, after a few moments, he jumps up, an excited little boy.

"I got it!" he cries, jubilant. "I got it down to three!" He mutters on his way to the blackboard, "It's *Pirke Avot*, I think, *Ethics of the Fathers*." Then he grabs the chalk and scrawls, speaking as he writes:

"Do justice.
Love kindness.
Walk humbly.

That is all that God requires of you." Laying down the chalk, he looks over at Carla. "How's that?" he asks.

To his amazement, she laughs at him. Her laughter is the same as usual, free and apparently friendly, but he looks at her uncertainly, not understanding, waiting for her to finish.

When she finally stops laughing, she explains. "That's way too easy!" she says. "*Anyone* can do *that*!"

At which he stares at her, even more astonished, and then bursts out laughing himself. He laughs till there are tears in his eyes. They are still there when the class is over, after he has thanked them, after they have risen to their feet and clapped.

Then he and Carla walk back to the house. The sun is setting, and on the way the rabbi nods to his congregants walking to *shul* for the evening prayers. He tells one of them that he will be along soon, and then he and Carla walk on in silence. She feels awkward with him now. She doesn't know what to call him, he is nameless to her. "Rabbi" is too formal, but his nickname Binny (Ricky's name for him, the diminutive of the Hebrew for Benjamin) feels too intimate.

"Do you want a sandwich?" she asks as they enter the house.

They pause together in the hall for a moment, absorbing its stillness.

"Sure," he says.

Then he asks her, as she's turning away, "Are you all right?"

She doesn't know what he means. In the daytime, she remembers nothing of her dreams, and almost nothing of his webbed shadow by her window. In the morning when she showers, it all washes away.

But now he has made her remember: the grape-smelling clam-
miness of her nightgown last night, the jagged cracks of sobbing
that woke him and then continued for some time even after he
shook her awake. He had asked, "Can I get you anything?" "I need
a new nightgown," she said, and he brought her one of Ricky's,
laid it at the end of her bed, a bright rectangle in the moonlight.
She peeled off the other one after he left, and felt the clean, dry
flannel, as comforting as a baby's sleeper, against her skin.

She shrugs. "I'm all right," she says, wanting to cry, and leaves
for the kitchen. A few minutes later, as she's standing at the
island, smearing mayonnaise on two pairs of sliced bread, she
hears soft footsteps behind her, then feels his hand touching hers
as he takes the knife out of her hand and gently lays it down. His
hands are around her waist and he is turning her around to face
him. She feels panicky, but she looks up at him. It is her rabbi, the
one who comes to comfort her in the night; and she watches,
mesmerized, as he takes her hand in his, and brings it to his lips.
He is kissing her hand in a stately, respectful way, and she thinks
of *She*, which they've just finished reading in school, as if she were
the queen, and he one of her subjects. His head is bent over her
hand, she feels the warm pressure of his lips. It looks like he is
worshipping: worshipping her, her mind, her youth—worshipping also her worship of him.

Now he turns over her hand. He is kissing her palm on the
inside—she is embarrassed, it is sweaty—and as she watches him,
hypnotized, he is kissing one of her fingers, slowly, gently, up the
whole length of it and then back down again. She hears the
beginning, rising wail of the tea kettle, she's forgotten about the
tea, she must turn it off. But she is frozen, watching in fascination, as though this has nothing to do with her, as though it is
happening to somebody else. His mouth moves over to her next

finger, and this one he is kissing with his lips, but also she feels something flicking, something light and sensual, like scurrying silk, it must be his tongue. And then she feels her finger going deep inside his mouth, and it is being sucked up-and-down, up and down, over and over. He starts to moan, no it is her that is moaning, and she feels her knees buckle under her. They are kneeling together on the kitchen floor, behind the island with the cutting board. The kettle is shrieking.

Suddenly Carla awakens as if from a trance, and with horror pulls away her hand. She looks at the rabbi: He is still back there in that other place, he is breathing heavily, and he won't look at her, he is looking down. Then somehow he has clasped her hands, both of them, in his, and he is holding them as if comforting one of his congregants, as if comforting a mourner, or a lost person. She hears the door to the kitchen opening somewhere behind her, and the next thing she knows, she is outside, she is on a bus, she is staring at her hands.

On the long ride home, she relives, over and over, the swelling tremor that started in her body, like the genesis of an earthquake, when she felt the licking flicking of his tongue up and down her finger; and then when he took it deep inside his mouth and sucked it, the caving-in, the landslide in her loins. But mingled with this is what she felt pulling her hand away, the most profound *No* she has ever uttered. The pleasure and the horror flip-flop within her, like two sides of the same hand, and by the time the bus has reached her parents' street, they have merged, like the inside and outside of skin.

She isn't ready to go home and face her parents, so she goes to the forest at the end of their street. It is a bright night lit by a glowing gold moon, and she sits on the ground, hugging her knees to her chest, surrounded by towering trees. Over the next few hours, the sound of the rushing traffic dies down; and by the time the silence of the night has entered the forest, she knows that there will be no more safety, and no more fathers, and no more hope for her, ever again. She knows now that the world is godless and empty, and there will be no redemption, not through the body, and not through the mind.

She doesn't know where she will sleep tonight. But she knows she will not go home; and for the first time ever, she has no words, no human words, for the knowledge in her heart. She raises her hands to her face and covers it, the way she does when blessing the candles to welcome in the Sabbath; and under the full moon she howls, together with the wolves, and all the other creatures of the forest, and the night.

Final Movement

"WHO IS BLESSED?" ASK the program notes. I am in a concert hall on a Saturday night in Winnipeg, and the choir, dressed in long white robes trimmed with red, is singing the first movement of a new Canadian piece called "Blessed."

"He who is content with his lot," the program notes answer, with thanks to Benjamin Franklin. "And who is content with his lot? Nobody."

Then, in an effort to be more contemporary, they also quote Simon & Garfunkel: "Blessed are the meek for they shall inherit. Blessed are the sat-upon, spat-upon, ratted-on. Oh Lord, why have you forsaken me?"

Blessed.

~

Blessed are those like Ruth, who was loved loved loved. Who glowed with love, looking up open-faced to everyone and anyone. Who knew so little of shame that she never even shut the bathroom door. What for? Her body wasn't dirty, there was nothing about her to be ashamed of. Pure, like loved light.

Every Saturday afternoon her mother braided her hair and tied the forest green sash on her plaid dress into a crisp big bow at the back. She did this with thoughtless love, like tying a bow on a gift before giving it away. (She was preparing to give Ruth to her father, the conductor of our local symphony, who took her along with him on Saturday afternoons to the Young People's Concerts.) I watched her tie Ruth's bow, and saw Ruth, with a thoughtlessness equal to her mother's, accept the gift in the bow: the love buried in it, like the music waiting silently in the bow of a violin when it isn't being played.

I watched, wishing Ruth's mother were my mother. Wishing she would braid my hair.

But I was seven years older, and only a kid in the neighbourhood who babysat for them from time to time. Her parents loved me a little bit, with what was left over from loving their own. (There was only Ruth when I met them, but I know there was an older daughter somewhere who had run away and no one ever talked about.) Still their love was something: A huge grey sweater urged on me as I left their house at night, its scratchy warmth against my skin as I walked the two blocks home in the cold darkness. My favourite cheese that they sometimes bought for me when they knew I was coming over to babysit—a wheel made up of twelve little triangles, each one individually wrapped with a picture of a cow on the front. And the gentle way Mrs. Barron at first asked after my sick mother's health; then when she died, how she said lightly, almost casually, "Don't be a stranger, you just come on by any time you feel like it. We're always happy to see you, and Ruthie loves you so."

Ruth looked up to me, she trusted me with the simple naiveté of the loved person, never suspecting anything but love. She liked me because she liked everybody; but also she admired me because I was seven years older, in high school, and already going out with boys. She came to me as to a big sister when, at the age of eleven, she had her first kiss. We sat on her bed, and she opened up her diary to where she had recorded the big event. On the left side of the page, she had written in huge capital letters MONTY, and on the page facing it, a fierce black scribble that had slightly ripped the page. "Remember," she asked, "that party I went to at Melinda's?" I nodded. "That's where Monty kissed me. My first kiss!" Then she laughed and blushed, a proud and pretty blush.

She came to me as to a big sister, to one who understands the ways of the world and can protect. I looked down into that trusting face as she showed me her diary, the closest she could come to a secret. I was amazed at her openness, and envious, too; but I couldn't help wondering what would happen to her when she went out into the world. I thought, panicking, *Someone needs to watch out for her.* Someone would need to shadow her through all her days, hiding a few feet behind her in bushes, like Miriam hid in the bulrushes to watch over Moses. I thought, with my teenage sophistication, that it would be me, that *I* would look out for her, *I* would be her guardian angel. I would extend my wing over her and protect her from harm.

But it has never been necessary. In all these years nothing bad has ever happened to her. She was blessed, she was loved from the day she was born. Life itself has been her angel.

◆◆◆

I am at this concert, back home after five years away. I come back only for deaths: for my uncles, and their wives, and my father.

~
81

And now for my father's only sister, my Auntie Phaedra, the last of them all. I was never particularly close to her, no one was; but she never married and there is nobody else, so it has been left to me to sort through her affairs. In her will she referred to me as her goddaughter, which is true, though I'd forgotten that—maybe because I've never felt any special connection to her. Though I do remember one time—I must have been about nine—when she took me to a Saturday afternoon concert. (I'm not sure how this happened—I think my parents had to go to a funeral or something, we had series tickets, so she offered to help out.) Ruth's father was conducting, as usual, and five singers in costume were singing excerpts from *The Magic Flute*.

Yesterday was the funeral. Today I saw the lawyer, and then paced senselessly around this town that used to be home to me, going up and down once-familiar streets, feeling lost and stunned. I have no friends here any more (they are all in Vancouver, like me, or Toronto), and now I have no family here, either: Next time I come back, *if* I ever come back, I will have to stay at a hotel. This trip I am staying at my aunt's, in her musty-smelling, death-filled house; and just to not have to go back there, at about 5:00 today I bought a paper, looking for somewhere to go. I saw the ad for this concert, came straight down here to the theatre, and got myself a ticket. *It is not wrong*, I tell myself. *After all, it is a concert of sacred music: the next best thing to a funeral.*

"Blessed" ends, thank God, and the mediocre red-and-white choir departs from the stage. Fortunately, this was only the appetizer: the main course of the evening is a prayer cycle, the latest composition by Tom Combes, the prodigious young composer whose name seems to be everywhere at once. His new piece, "God's Love Revealed," is dedicated to the great contralto, Greta

Himmelfarb, who will be performing it tonight for its world premiere. I smile to myself, remembering Tom as he was before he was anybody famous, when he and Ruth first started going out: two kids, very young and innocent, a first love for them both. Tom was skinny, and shy, and as pale as a saint. He had come to Winnipeg from a small Manitoba town, the son of a choirmaster, to study composition at the Conservatory. Back then he went by Thomas, not Tom: a Catholic boy struggling with his faith, something that I, with my secular background, found ludicrous (what was there to struggle with, after all?). But his brilliance, his tormented brilliance, was immediately recognized by Ruth's father, the head of the Conservatory at that time. He took Tom under his wing, and the young protégé began to spend evenings at the Barrons', then weekends, and after that, virtually all his spare time. Within a few months, however, he was coming not to sit in the living room with his mentor, listening to him pontificate with his feet up on a stool, about their shared love, sacred music; he was coming for Ruth. To go for walks with her. To hold her hand. Then to ask for it in marriage.

Now Bruno Barron sweeps on to the stage, thunderously impatient as usual, as if he is far too busy for this kind of trivia; and frowning, he bows curtly to the audience, as though even this small gesture is more than we deserve. But now from the right, Tom joins him on the stage, and the old lion smiles a real smile, beams at his son-in-law, extends a hand to him, and when Tom takes it, holds it up in the air, like indicating the champion in a boxing match. Tom has changed: he is older, his body has filled out. He is still tall, but slim rather than skinny, and the gangly awkwardness is gone. Success has done well by him. Or maybe it is Ruth's love that has given him this confidence. Whatever it is, he's a man now. (He looks around thirty-five, which is about right: he's one year older than Ruth.) Then Tom and his father-in-law bow to each other ceremoniously, and the audience goes wild clapping and cheering. One misguided man shouts "Bravo!" as though they have already played Tom's piece. (Or maybe it doesn't matter to him; maybe he loves it on principle.) I have forgotten, being away, what a cult figure Ruth's father is, and it is my first exposure to the worship accorded Tom, as to the heir-apparent in a dynasty. Suddenly I am weary, terribly weary: *Vanity, vanity. All is vanity.* I remember the funeral—the dust of the earth, the hardness of the earth, as the spade tried to bite its first bite. Ashes to ashes, dust to dust.

Tom's new piece is not bad at all, in contrast to the others I've heard: two on the CBC a couple of years back, and one performed in Vancouver last fall. They were cold, as cold as death. "Cold fire," Steven Sandbagge wrote in the *Vancouver Sun*: a nice turn of phrase but, like "passionately religious" (also in Sandbagge's review), meaningless to me, not something that I can understand. I never could see what others saw in Tom's music: why everywhere he's gone it's been nothing but praise, praise, praise. "He has the power and purity of a modern young prophet," gushed a review in *The New York Times* two months ago, after his choral suite was first performed at Carnegie Hall. "Combes' music makes accessible to the contemporary listener all the agony and ecstasy of the religious life. He has truly created an ascetic aesthetic."

But now through this piece I can see a little of what they mean. Or maybe it is just Greta Himmelfarb and her incredible charisma and artistic power. Her eyes are closed and she seems completely entranced as she sings, "God Himself has kissed each blade of grass." She has a wonderful, throaty, melodious voice (the "Himmelfarb texture"), and at forty-five is at the peak of her powers and celebrity: Just last month she was awarded the coveted Deutschegrammafon Gamma, and was the unanimous first choice of all the judges. Through her voice you can feel Tom's religious longings straining against, then breaking through, the restraints of the traditional form. She is also beautiful to look at. Her chestnut hair is piled up on the top of her head, and she is wearing a tight, strapless silver dress completely thatched in shiny metal sequins, like hundreds of tiny scales; the way it flares out at the bottom around her feet, she looks like a shapely and voluptuous mermaid, half of this world, half of another. She is nothing short of magnificent.

She finishes singing: the piece is over. A standing ovation, howls of "Bravo!" and "Bis!" and then three encores, the last one a replaying of the final movement. Greta and Barron each bow; then Barron beckons to Tom, who comes on stage again to thunderous applause. Barron and Tom both reach out to Greta, she takes their hands, and with her in the middle, the three of them bow together. Barron then goes over and shakes the hand of the curly-haired first violin, whom I recognize suddenly as Henry Hailik from my high school days. Again enthusiastic applause (someone whistles); and in a dramatic gesture, Barron has the whole symphony rise to its feet and bow.

During the intermission it is crowded backstage, and although I can see Tom, I can't get anywhere near him. He is surrounded, almost crushed, by five layers deep of admirers and fans, and all I can see of him is the short tawny hair at the back of his head. Over near the door another fan cluster is fast forming: the Maestro has entered the backstage area and is instantly surrounded. *I have to get out of here,* I think, panicking, almost unable to breathe. I turn around quickly and crash right into Henry

Hailik. The people he is standing with glare at me, but Henry only laughs.

"It's you!" he cries, facing me, and turning his back to the others. "I thought I saw you in the audience. What a gorgeous dress."

I feel myself flush all the way up my neck. I am wearing a joyous springtime dress, full of reds and oranges and pinks. Not at all the thing for one day after a funeral, but it's what I put on when I got up this morning. To make matters worse, he then asks,

"What are you doing in town?"

I tell him about my aunt.

"Not again," he says. "You and your funerals. Is that the only way we can get you back home for a visit?"

I remember now that a couple of visits back (I think I was here for my father), I ran into Henry in the park with his little boy, and we chatted briefly near the swings. I am with an old friend—at last some evidence that I did live here once, that my childhood, my growing-up, my formative years did really happen. Henry smiles at me, and I feel a physical rush of warmth and happiness. For the first time during this visit, things feel a little bit right.

"You're first violin now, I see," is what I say to Henry. "That's great."

He shrugs and smiles. "I can't complain. And you? What are you doing these days?"

"I'm still at the Vancouver Museum," I say. "I'm head now of Contemporary Exhibits."

"That's right, I think I heard that from Mick..."

He starts telling me about my cousin Mick who lives in Ottawa, and how Mick came backstage a few months ago when Henry was at the National Arts Centre performing with the symphony. They hadn't seen each other since high school, they used to play hockey together...I am beginning to feel vague again, he is drifting away from me, where is that vivid, real feeling of a moment ago?

Then the lights start flashing, and Henry leans toward me.

"Listen," he says, "what are you doing after the concert?"

"Nothing much."

"What do you say we go out for a drink? We could talk some more, catch up a little bit. It's been so long."

I hesitate. Then I shrug. "Sure, why not?"

"Great," he says. "Meet you here when it's over?"

I'm in the middle of nodding but he's already gone, running inside.

⊷≡◉≡⊶

The second half of the concert I can't even tell you what they are playing. At the end of the intermission I rushed back to my seat, and did not even have time to pick my program up off the floor and see what I would be listening to. I hardly hear the music, anyway; all I am aware of is Henry, whom I stare at unapologetically: *I'm allowed to be watching him. People come to concerts to watch the musicians play. He must be used to it by now.* I notice how Henry's hair still flips upwards over his ears, the same as it did back then; and all of a sudden he looks eighteen years old again: the age when he graduated and disappeared off to college, while I was still in high school two grades behind him. We all knew he was talented, but he wasn't weird or anything, he wasn't always rushing home to practise like Abner Moser, whose mother wanted him to be a child prodigy. Henry was normal: he played hockey after school like all the guys, and he looked and acted like everyone else. Not awkward or deathly pale like Tom. Though Ruth never seemed to mind; to her these were marks of Tom's sensitivity, his specialness. That's how it is with a girl in love: even the defects, the thorns, become jewels in the crown.

I remember the first time I heard Ruth speak Tom's name. It was on one of my first visits back (I think that time it was for my Uncle Harry), I was already living in Vancouver where I was doing a Masters in Fine Arts; and I was over at Ruth's parents' for one of their afternoon musicales. They had a young up-and-coming tenor there who was passing through town on his first national tour, accompanied by a nervous friend with a straggly red beard. The tenor sang for us in a strong, unsubtle voice—some of Schubert's *lieder*, and the drinking song from *Das Lied von der Erde*, which we all very much enjoyed. Then we moved into the dining room and sat around the table for coffee and pastries and fruit and cheese. As if I were still their babysitter, or an adopted daughter, I helped Ruth's mother serve the two guests, carrying in milk and sugar, and cups of coffee, and replenishing the apples and grapes.

It was a soft spring day with the late afternoon sun splashing all over the table. On my left, past Ruth who sat in the last seat, were two glass doors opening out onto the porch, and I felt suddenly imprisoned, longing to be free and outside on this beautiful day. From the porch came the sounds that since childhood I have always associated with spring: drilling and hammering, the sounds of construction. But this time the drilling was very loud and disturbing, like the drilling at a dentist's, and the conversation around the table was like the meaningless, fearful small talk before the dentist begins to drill.

Because always, always in this house, the guests were drilled.

"So," said Barron to the tenor, when everyone had had something to eat and drink. "What are your plans after Winnipeg?"

The young man talked about the remainder of his tour. Barron tore apart the conductors he would be working with in each of the coming cities.

Then the tenor said:

"After this is all done, I'm going to look into learning some contemporary repertoire. Have you heard of Pete Porter's work out in Victoria? It sounds like he's doing some interesting stuff."

Barron looked down at his plate. There was a short pause like a pause note.

"Nonsense," he said. "A waste of your time."

The tenor looked up at Barron surprised, as though he couldn't believe he had heard quite right. But even so he blushed and his voice was a little unsteady when he answered.

"I think that some of what's happening in contemporary music in this country is really quite important. We owe it to ourselves to take it a little more seriously, to try and understand it."

"We owe ourselves nothing," said Barron contemptuously, staring down the tenor. "We owe the past, we owe the great masters. To know them and play them as they deserve to be played. We don't need new scales, and tricks, and 'musical languages.' What was good enough for Schubert is good enough for me. Or perhaps you are saying, young man, that you think Pete Porter superior to Schubert?"

"I'm not saying—"

"Enough!" shouted the conductor, his face suddenly red. "Enough!" And he brought his hand down on the table like the final note of a symphony.

There was silence. The tenor did not try again. His hand trembled as he raised his fork halfway to his mouth and then set it down again. His friend's face began to twitch. My heart was pounding, I didn't know where to look. Staring into the white tablecloth, I felt myself being swallowed up into the endless silence, sucked deeper and deeper into its vortex. Helpless, I waited for the silence to end, for words to return things to normal.

And then a voice piped up, innocent and cheerful: "Does anybody know a good movie? Tommy and I are going out tonight, but we don't know what to see."

Astonished, I turned to my left and looked at Ruth. She was sitting at the end of the table, bathed in the sun flooding in through the glass doors. She sat in the midst of this destruction, in the midst of a kind of terror, oblivious to it all. Her chin on her hand, she added dreamily,

"Something nice. Something romantic..."

That face, I will never forget it as long as I live: the face of the quintessential girl in love—glowing, knowing, knowing nothing but love. The tenor's friend answered her, and I watched his lips move as he spoke; but it was like watching a movie with the sound turned off: I couldn't hear a thing. All I heard, over and over, was Ruth's childish, hopeful voice: "Something nice, something romantic." As if I could, by repeating her words over and over in my head, learn like her to see only love.

⸱⸱✦◉✦⸱⸱

Ruth and Tom were married within the year. Of course. If Ruth loved, naturally she was loved back: it was as inevitable as the theme of a sonatina returning at the end. None of the longing and yearning and fractured love that formed the emotional core of my young womanhood. The wedding took place in a charming old chapel on the outskirts of Winnipeg, and everybody who was anybody in Manitoba music was there. As they stood before the priest, Tom and Ruth looked remarkably like the wedding picture of her parents that Ruth kept on her desk: the hopeful, brilliant young prodigy looking off into the future; and his tender trusting bride looking up at him. I attended the wedding without an escort, wandering around at loose ends, trying not to look lonely. The older sister, and unmarried. I ate and ate and then went home. That night I slept with the man I had been too embarrassed to bring along: a simple, good-hearted man named Bob, the carpenter who had come to fix my bookshelves. And because I'd been ashamed to be seen with him, I was also ashamed when we slept together, as though I had been unfaithful to everyone who mattered to me, all in one single night.

I got married a year later in Vancouver, to an engineer from there named Darrell; and in about the third year of our marriage, around the time I was starting my job as assistant to the curator at the Vancouver Museum, Ruth and Tom passed through town. Tom had a conference on sacred music, and Ruth came along because she had never been to Vancouver. I remember being nervous that they wouldn't like what I had prepared (hamburgers on the barbecue, a macaroni salad, and strawberry pie). Darrell laughed at me for being nervous, and we had a huge fight just before they arrived. But it all worked out fine. They did like the food, and much to my relief Tom and Darrell hit it off, in that male competitive sort of way. Afterwards Ruth and I cleaned up together in the kitchen, and without meaning to hurt me (I'm sure she didn't mean to, how could she know I was having trouble getting pregnant?), she said that she wasn't a "career woman" like me, she just wanted to have a lot of kids. When I saw her again, the last time, three years after that, she already had a one- and a two-year-old. I was back for my Uncle Arthur's funeral, and it was also the first time I'd brought Darrell home. It was a hot summer afternoon, and he and I sat with Ruth and Tom on their patio, sipping lemonade and eating canapés off a tray, while their two daughters played quietly beside us on the grass. At one point we were interrupted by a student of Tom's coming around the back to drop something off. Tom was annoyed at being disturbed on the weekend. "You could have left it at my office," he said sharply, and the boy started to stammer and left in a hurry. I looked at Ruth, but her face was placid, untroubled. She was standing—so pretty in a white summer dress—holding out a platter of canapés to Tom, and he helped himself while continuing to talk to Darrell without even looking up at her.

That was seven years ago, and I've had no contact with Ruth or Tom since. Except for the time I called them from the airport, when I was switching planes in Winnipeg, just to say I was passing through. But I have, of course, heard over the years of Tom's meteoric rise. I have also heard about the Maestro, whose affairs by now are common knowledge: he has become so open about them that last year he even showed up on opening night with his mistress of the month on his arm. This morning's gossip column noted that every day this week he has sent a dozen red roses to Greta Himmelfarb's dressing room—as embarrassing to me as if he and I were related. And in my own marriage, no affairs but no happiness between us either: a vast emptiness, a well that can't be filled. Maybe children would have helped, who knows? But one is blessed or one isn't, and there is nothing one can do about that. It is years now since Darrell and I first recognized, acknowledged our unhappiness out loud to each other; and it has lain between us ever since, like a smelly yellow dog half-asleep on the floor between our two chairs, as we grow old in front of the fire. It is relatively undisruptive, just unwilling to move; it will be with us forever, I suppose.

Sometimes in the middle of the night, when I can't stand the loneliness any more, when I am sure I can't survive one more day without love, I wonder what I would be like, what my life would be like, if when I was a little girl, I had been loved. Really loved, the way a child is supposed to be. And of course I think then of Ruth, with her round glowing cheeks and her ribbons and her bows; and also of her brilliant, charismatic husband and her patio and two daughters on the grass. At these times, when I am scared or lost, and fear that really there is nothing, nothing one can really believe in or count on, nothing that *continues*, I think of Ruth and Tom. And then I know that the world does go on: that at least on one little island, something makes sense, things are the way they are supposed to be, it has all worked out.

-·-▭◉▭-·-

After the concert Henry says, "Let's go for a walk," and he takes my elbow in the old-fashioned way, and we walk arm-in-arm through the almost-empty theatre, like a couple strolling on a boardwalk somewhere in old Europe on a spring day before the war, on Somethingstrasse. But when we get to the door of the theatre, we see it is raining outside, so we hurry into Henry's shabby green car, and just drive back to my aunt's house for a drink. The rain runs down the car windows in rivulets; they join together at the bottom like fingers connecting to form a hand. Henry fiddles with the radio once or twice, but because of the rainstorm nothing comes through but static. I don't feel much like talking, and apparently neither does he; so we drive in silence, watching the rain.

My aunt's house is old and Gothic, and has always felt a little spooky, even when she lived there. But now as we approach it, turrets and all in the middle of a thunderstorm, it looks like the setting for a horror movie; and the front door actually creaks when I open it to let Henry in. Once inside the hallway, I am still shuddering from the chill of the rain; I shrug off my coat, its wet wool smelling like a half-drowned sheep, and throw it carelessly over the bannister. Henry does the same with his, imitating my gesture exactly, and his coat lands on top of mine. We grin at each other. Then he notices the gargoyles and cuckoo clocks and red china devils on the shelves above the doorways, and then past them, all the way up, the high gabled ceiling.

"Some house," he says.

"Yeah, I know. Come, let's have a drink."

I lead the way through the living room to my aunt's liquor cabinet, with Henry following close behind and looking up and around at everything as he walks. My aunt drank primarily "ladies' drinks," so in the cabinet there is plenty of Amaretto and crème de menthe and peach liqueur. Henry points to the crème de menthe; I pour it out for him into an ample brandy snifter. I drink peach liqueur myself, picturing my aunt, becoming my aunt as I drink it, drinking her, drinking up her lonely life. And then I do something my aunt would never have done. I take Henry's hand and lead him up the stairs to the bedroom, to my aunt's room, which I have been using for my own. We sit on the edge of the soft old featherbed, on a down quilt with a picture of a butterfly on it, and with my legs tucked under me, and Henry's stretched out straight in front of him, peacefully we sip our drinks. It all feels very high school, maybe because our drinks are syrupy green and orange, which reminds me of "going for a soda"; maybe because I suddenly feel terribly self-conscious about my body in a way that I haven't for years. I don't feel at all like I am forty-one years old, or the chief curator of the Vancouver Museum; and especially not like someone who has been married for sixteen years. I am a young girl again: not really like I ever actually was; more the way I could have been, should have been, if I hadn't been so busy taking care of my mother and my dad. Now they are both dead, anyway; and so is my aunt. The very last one of their generation, the last death, the final death, the death of deaths. Now, finally, I am sixteen and free. Sitting next to a boy, happy that he likes me. Hoping to be loved.

Henry finishes drinking and puts his glass down on the floor. Then he takes my almost-finished drink out of my hand and places it gently next to his. Now he takes me in his arms and we lie back on my aunt's bed, and he kisses me very softly on the lips, like testing them, testing their softness. Then a harder one, like testing for strength: His tongue opens my mouth, and he kisses me passionately everywhere inside. Then he kisses me one more time, this time as gently as a butterfly.

I just lie there in a kind of trance. It has been so long since anyone but Darrell has kissed me, I had forgotten (I hadn't really thought about it at all) how different Henry's kiss would be from Darrell's. How every man's kiss is different from every other man's, more unique than a snowflake. As soft as a snowflake Henry's closing kiss: a snowflake melting at the corner of my lip.

"I always liked you," he says to me, stroking my hair. It feels so beautiful, it makes me want to cry.

"I liked you, too," I say, trying to keep my voice normal, and failing. "But you were older, I thought you didn't even notice me."

"I noticed you. I used to see you at the Saturday afternoon concerts, but I didn't have the guts to come over."

I stare at him in amazement, but he has said this with a totally straight face. "You used to wear this red pleated skirt," he adds.

I haven't thought of that skirt in twenty-five years, but I remember it perfectly. It had a matching red jacket and was the only outfit that I had for concerts. I look at Henry, and strangely moved, I reach up and touch his cheek.

"I want to make love to you," he whispers.

I lower my eyes, frightened by his directness. *What am I afraid of?* I wonder as I lie there, and tenderly, respectfully, he kisses my ear, my neck, my shoulder. Is it losing my virginity I'm worried about? Is this part of feeling sixteen again—this return to high school morality, with its bourgeois good-girl stuff? All that anguish over "To fuck or not to fuck"! I don't believe that nonsense, or at least I don't think I do. After all, I am forty-one years old, and a feminist. And yet maybe I still am a virgin, in a certain sense: despite all the unhappiness in our marriage, I have never yet been unfaithful to Darrell. Henry kisses my mouth and runs his fingers lightly over my breasts. It feels so wonderful. And I am getting older: in a few years, perhaps, I'll have no more interest in sex at all. I could even be dead. Why deprive myself of pleasure now? It won't hurt anybody; and I deserve some tenderness, some love.

I love the way he is touching me: softly, shyly, like a boy touching a girl for the very first time; and it makes me feel like it is my first time being touched. As if it matters, like it mattered back in high school, to touch somebody, to touch their body.

I want to tell Henry how I feel. I try to catch his eye, but he is intent on unbuttoning the buttons of my blouse.

"Henry?" I ask; and he answers by saying my name, echoing exactly my pleading tone, like a musical phrase repeated on another instrument. I laugh in spite of myself, even though I know that he is mocking me. That this is probably what he does whenever a woman tries to get close to him by saying his name in that wheedling, hopeful way. He wheedles her back, he throws her back onto herself, like throwing a shoe onto a mountain of shoes.

He has succeeded in opening my blouse, and now his hand is inside my bra, and he is doing the most exquisite things to my nipple. I arch my back and moan; and at the same time, I feel mild surprise at what is going on. That really, he really is expecting me to take off my clothes, peel everything off, including my underpants (even the doctor lets you keep your panties on) and let him, a complete stranger (because that is what he is, even if he *feels* familiar) put his hand there, on my clitoris, and touch it; and then I am supposed to spread my legs and let him stick his penis in.

"Henry," I say.

I touch his hand and then take it out of my bra. He smiles down at me—sweetly, like a child, as if he expected to be stopped and just wanted to see how far he could go.

"Could we talk a little?" I ask.

"What?" he says teasingly. "You can't talk while I'm touching you? You can't concentrate?"

"No," I smile.

"All right then. What do you want to talk about?"

"Oh, I don't know." I think for a moment. "Tell me what you think of Tom Combes. Do you think he's talented? Did you like his latest piece?"

"Oh, he's talented all right," says Henry.

But there's something in his tone, something he's not saying, that makes me curious.

"What?" I ask. "Come on, tell me what you're thinking. Tell me the truth."

"Well, it doesn't hurt that he's Barron's son-in-law," says Henry. I smile appreciatively. "Or," he adds, "that he's Greta Himmelfarb's lover—what is it? What's wrong?"

I have spun over to the other side of the bed, and I am lying curled up like a baby, with my back to him.

"I'm sorry. I thought you knew."

Tom. Greta Himmelfarb's lover. Tom, Greta's lover. Tom has a lover.

"I was sure you knew. Everybody knows."

Everybody but me. Everybody but Ruth. Someone must tell her, someone must let her know. I am panting, I can't seem to catch my breath.

Ruth and Tom. Tom and Greta...

A voice, far away, has said something, but I didn't hear what it was.

"What?"

"You and Tom, did you have a relationship?"

"What?" I say again. I roll back over and face Henry, who is looking at me with concern. I understand his question now, and I look back at him to answer, without trying to hide the pain that is flooding me, that I'm sure shows on my face.

"No," I tell him. "I knew Ruth growing up. She's like a little sister to me."

"I'm sorry, I didn't realize..."

I nod dumbly, unable to speak again.

Ruth's trusting face as she showed me her diary. *What will happen to a person like this in the world?*

Henry reaches out and touches my arm. I am numb: I can see that he is touching me, but I don't feel a thing. I can't feel anything because nothing means anything. Nothing makes any sense. Then Henry takes me in his arms again, but I am like a rag doll: I don't resist but also I can't participate. It isn't the same as before. Nothing is going to be the same ever again.

⋯→▬◉▬←⋯

After Henry is gone I lie in my bed, naked, for a long time, watching the rain and the lightning, counting the seconds between the lightning and the thunder. At around two-thirty I realize I am not going to fall asleep, so I get out of bed and climb the rickety winding steps to the attic. The lawyer has said that my aunt's "personal effects" are up there, that I am free to look through them and see if there is anything I want to keep. The attic is panelled entirely with planks of miscellaneous wood in all different shades, from yellow to almost black, and it is so dusty that I begin to sneeze. I am about to go back down when I notice over in the corner an old steamer trunk, the kind my cousin and I used to imagine was a chest of buried treasure, full of pearl necklaces and rubies and gold. I kneel in front of it and push back the heavy lid. Inside there are three piles of neatly stacked clothing. (*How like my aunt,* I think, *to bury her treasures like so much folded laundry!*) From the left-hand pile, I pull off the top garment: something light blue and long and lacy. But like a magician's scarf, it seems to have no end: I pull and pull at it, whatever it is, and it unravels and unravels until I finally reach the end of it and the whole first pile in the trunk is gone. It is a strange, old shawl: I stand up and fling it over my shoulder with flair, as if I am Isadora Duncan and this, one of her romantic, deadly scarves. But then, because it is so long, I keep winding it around my neck and scalp and face; and by the time I finish, this ancient thing is covering my whole head, like the bindings of a mummy—even my mouth. As if my aunt's voice has soaked into it over time, and is mutely whispering: "Don't let anyone kiss you, dear."

I make a space for my eyes, and kneel again over the contents of the chest. Then I reach inside and touch something white on the top of the middle pile. I am surprised, even shocked, knowing my aunt as I do, at the soft feel of satin. The satiny thing unfolds into a negligee, innocent and pure and white—except for a small pink embroidered rose where the fabric dips into the V of the breasts—as translucent as the moon on a quiet night. Something for a wedding night, or a young girl dreaming of love. *What is this doing in my aunt's chest?* I realize suddenly how little I really know of my aunt, how little any of us knew. Did she have a lover—or lovers—that nobody knew anything about? Romantic dinners, long nights of love, right here in this Gothic house? It's possible, I suppose. Hard to imagine after all these years of seeing her as an old maid. But possible. She *could* have worn this negligee—why not? anyone can wear a negligee—and it obviously belonged to her (what else would it be doing here?).

Then again, maybe she bought it but never wore it—she

might have been saving it, hoping the time would come when it would be needed. (I can see her buying it on sale somewhere, thinking, *Well, sooner or later I may have occasion for something like this*.) Perhaps she tried it on now and then in front of her mirror, just to feel its softness, just to feel beautiful, here where no one could laugh at her, my big-boned, unloved aunt. Or maybe all she did was finger it once in a while, stroking its smoothness with secret longing but never daring to try it on.

I unwind the long blue scarf, drop it on the floor, and try on the negligee. It fits almost perfectly. Underneath, remembering Henry's fingers, my breasts still feel alive and sensitive, especially the left one, which has always been bigger than the other, but now is swollen to even larger than its usual size. Lightly I stroke it and watch the little nipple rise, showing rose-like through the milky satin.

I wish Henry were here to see.

Like Tom watching Greta: I can imagine her modeling her negligees for him. But none of this sweetness and innocence for her: red satin, with a bodice as tight-fitting as a bathing suit and red lace around the breasts. Tom stares at her. Then he reaches out his right hand and with half-shut eyes, places it over Greta's left breast, which is voluptuously protruding from the lace. If he closes his hand and turns it sharply to the right, it will be the exact same gesture as picking an apple off a tree.

Someone must tell Ruth. I must warn her: she must know. I see myself rushing over to her house, standing with her in her front yard near the apple tree and the little picket fence, earnestly telling her The Truth. But will she be happy, grateful? Will that make us like sisters again? Of course not. She won't believe me, she will suspect my motives. Why would I say such a horrible thing to her, why am I trying to hurt her? And of course she'll ask: "Where did you hear this? Who told you?" And then what am I supposed to say? "I heard it from Henry Hailik, while we were in bed together almost-making-love"? "Who is Henry Hailik?" she'll ask, even though she knows him from the symphony. "What does *he* know? Did he see them together in bed?" No, she won't say that. She'll tell me she knows her Tommy and he would never in a million years do anything like that. He is a *spiritual* man, anguished by his alienation from God, a composer of sacred music.

She will tell me to go away and never to darken her doorstep again.

All right. I strip off the negligee and sit down naked on the attic floor. *Fine.* I, too, will be complicit. I, like everyone else in Winnipeg, will know and keep silent: will watch Ruth come and go, live her life, and I will say and do nothing. As silent as a cloud.

Fine.

But then I am suddenly furious at all these people, laughing at Ruth behind her back, while to her face they treat her with respect: *Bruno Barron's daughter, Tom Combes' wife.* And she, oblivious, struts around like a princess, pitying others less fortunate than herself: lonely women like my aunt, and women in unhappy marriages, like me, and divorcees. By comparison we all make her glow. She walks around thinking that she is blessed, that as the sun shines down on her, she shines down on other people. When really no sun shines on her at all: just the thin, false light of a sixty-watt bulb.

It's all Tom's fault. And I hate him for it. I hate him. I hate his hypocrisy: the holy man, the bringer of sacred music to the soul-starved secular world. The liar. The phony. And I hate how men can do this, how men have the power to do this, to do whatever they want with women. Sure, the odd woman does it too, like

Greta; but how are such women usually looked at? Sluts. Whores. But not Tom, or Barron, when they are found out. On the contrary, other men grudgingly, some even openly, admire them for it. "Didn't know he had it in him, the bugger," they would be saying now of Tom. "A real man. Not some wimp, like most of these musicians." And even some women would approve: to them he would suddenly be more exciting, more attractive. The great composer. Needing comfort, needing love...

And I'm furious now also at Ruth—for being so naive, so sexually inexperienced, so virginal. So pure. Damn her innocence, damn her goddam purity. What is wrong with her that she doesn't know how to keep her man from wandering off? Why doesn't she know how to keep him happy? And why the hell can't she see what's going on?

I hear a tearing sound, and with surprise I look down at my lap. Without knowing it, I have picked my aunt's shawl up from the floor, dug my fingers into it, and yanked. The fine lace is ripped now, ripped irreparably like a huge gouge in the middle of a spider's web, so that there is no way ever to repair this antique and priceless thing. I look at the shawl, and scream. I scream and scream, *a madwoman in the attic,* and when I am all screamed out, I start to cry. I cry for a long time, curled up on the floor, clutching part of the shawl to my cheek. He shouldn't have told me, Henry, as though it were nothing, just a minor piece of gossip— when really it was the end of something, the breaking off of a piece of my world. Nothing is ever going to be all right again, nothing will ever be intact. I bring the shawl up to my nose, and inhale its comforting, familiar smell: the smell of musk, and old age, and my Auntie Phaedra. I doze off to the smell of once-was, never-again-shall-be.

I wake up cold and aching from sleeping on the floor and like an old woman, edge my way backwards down the attic stairs, like climbing down a ladder. At the bottom, the clock on the night-table says five. My teeth are chattering and my feet are cold on the linoleum floor. Quickly I crawl under the quilt with the butterfly on it, and pull around me its downy softness. Then I turn onto my right side and stare at the empty half of the bed. There is room there for a couple. For Tom and Greta. I can imagine them lying under a butterfly quilt like mine, touching and kissing each other on the hair, the face, the neck. Then they kick the quilt off, and I see them naked. Their bodies are glowing and golden, their legs are intertwined, and they are beautiful, knowing nothing but their own desire. His hand runs down her breast, over her hipbone, down her thigh. She trembles. He caresses her between her legs, and she moans; he climbs on top of her and slides inside her and quickly, within seconds, they both cry out. Then he falls into her arms, and like this they are instantly asleep.

I wish they were here—then I would roll over to their side of the bed, and snuggle up between them like a baby or a pet dog, just to feel against me the warmth of their sleeping skin. But as it is I get out of bed, go down to the kitchen, and make some coffee. This takes a while, since I have barely used the kitchen these last two days, and now I have to find where my aunt keeps things. (No, I correct myself, *kept*, where she *kept* things). And she doesn't keep (she didn't keep) things where I would: her mind works (worked) differently. An old metal coffeepot with a dent in the side, the kind I see nowadays only on camping trips, is located among the pots and pans. I pull off the top. It still smells of fresh coffee as if she brewed some just a few days ago, maybe enough for me too, hoping I would come for a visit. But I didn't. Well, here I am now, ready to drink. (But where are you, Auntie Phaedra?)

I find the coffee and a spoon. I measure the coffee out into the coffee pot, and add the water, and place the pot on a burner, and turn on the gas flame. Then, while it is beginning to bubble and perk its way into life, filling this old yellowed-walled kitchen with its strong brave smell, I sit down at the table—exhausted, as though instead of just turning on a stove, I have gathered and chopped wood, and done all the work of building a fire. I place my forehead straight down on the table's cool oilcloth, like a Moslem hitting his head on the ground in prayer: *Accept it— Power runs the world. All those other things—Morality, Gentleness, Love—they're nothing. Just toys. Toys for children like Ruth who have never grown up, and don't want to see the world as it really is. Toys for the powerful, too—to play with for as long as they're useful, and then toss aside. All that matters is power. If you have it, you take whatever you want from the world, you rob routinely from the weak and the meek. That's the way it is.*

I stay with my forehead on the table for quite some time, as if this humble posture will help me to accept what I know to be true. It also feels good to rest my head, to let go of its weight, knowing there is nowhere lower that it can fall.

Then I hear my aunt's voice.

"All right, that's enough of that," she says briskly. "Come on now. Snap out of it. Stop being such a baby."

Automatically I sit straight up, with the reflex of a repri-manded child.

"It's not the end of the world," she says. "Adults sometimes do this. They sleep with someone they're not married to. They're lonely, they need love—and they take it where they can find it."

"But it's wrong."

My aunt sighs. "Wrong. Right. Who knows what these things mean? I always did the 'right' thing. I was a good girl, did as I was told (not like your father, may I add). But how does that saying go—'You only go around once.' I didn't learn that till it was far too late."

She pauses. I feel confused hearing this from my aunt, and can't think of anything to say.

"Life is very hard," she adds, and sighs again. But then she speaks up brightly, as if ruled even now by the conventions of a lifetime: *You don't leave someone with a sad taste in the mouth.* In a perfect hostess voice, as though she is helping out at a symphony fundraising tea, my Auntie Phaedra says to me:

"Would you care for some coffee?"

And then she's gone.

⋆⇒◉⇐⋆

I get up and pour myself a cup. There is no milk, so I drink my coffee strong and black and bitter. And almost instantaneously, my eyes jerk open wide. With the clarity of caffeine, I can see exactly what my aunt was driving at.

He's still wrong, Tom. And I still hate him for what he's done. (I probably always will.) But also I can see that, in a way, this thing with Greta is probably the best thing that ever could have happened to him. I can feel for him, knowing a little bit about him from things that Ruth has let drop. So hard to be a good Catholic boy. To grow up with strict parents who never kissed or held you—never even a touch on the arm. The loneliness of it: for all your childhood to know no body but your own. And then in adolescence, to be painfully shy: to walk a girl all the way home and then not even dare to ask for a kiss. To know that the girls all laugh at you behind your back. Then, miraculously, you find love: A lovely girl, a warm and pretty girl, the daughter of a famous man, returns your love, and you marry with hope. Only to discover that she is just a person; and that sooner than you would have believed possible, her body becomes so familiar it feels almost like your own. And that loneliness comes roaring back, that craving for more, for closeness, for contact with another. You begin to think about making love only to this one woman for the rest of your life, and it feels to you like a kind of poverty, a return to something you thought you had escaped.

Years of disappointment, and longing, shame, and inner struggle. Finally Tom gives in. Half-believing that for this he will burn in eternal flames, he makes love to another woman. Afterwards he lies in Greta's soft white arms, overcome with gratitude and joy. He had never known such sensations before, things he had only caught glimpses of through movies and magazines, wondering if he would ever experience them himself. His Ruth, so good and affectionate—I can see exactly how she would make love to him: in a warm, wholehearted way, just like giving one of her daughters a hug. But sensuality? Sexuality? Knowing her own body, and his, and their potential for pleasure when brought together? Ruth knows nothing about this. Or how to create desire, the way Greta does, running one long fingernail, slowly, down the length of Tom's body. Then touching him all over, missing nothing (not an elbow, not the back of a knee), and kissing him everywhere too, in many different ways. Leisurely at first, then speeding up; pausing a little, then again building up the speed. Then, when he can't possibly want her any more than he does, she draws it out, she makes him wait, like pulling back a taut slingshot one inch more. He thinks that he is going to die. "I am going to die," he whispers to her; and only then does she lightly, elegantly (as elegantly as lifting a finger and letting a stone fly) release him.

Then he lies in her arms, trembling, and he thinks: *Now I am alive.* (He was only half-alive before, he sees that now: all these years he has been asleep, just waiting.) And to feel like this again, so deeply, truly alive, he will do anything. Anything. Including lie to Ruth, which he has done with gradually increasing regularity, until now it is almost easy for him to do—he who as a boy was caught whenever he told a lie, and whipped, because he couldn't lie without his voice cracking. Sometimes he thinks of confessing to Ruth, just blurting out the truth to her. *But what would be the point of that?* he argues with himself. *It would only hurt her, and for what?* (He is going, of course, to keep on seeing Greta, there is no real question about that.) And he still loves Ruth; in a strange way this has made him love her even more. Gone are the resentments for all the things she can't give him, for the dullness in her (not only in her body, but also in her mind), especially since the girls were born. Now he feels a particular tenderness for her. He is kind to her, the way you are kind to someone when you know you have the power to destroy them, and you decide, daily, not to.

Four years ago, that time I called them up from the Winnipeg airport, Ruth answered the phone. A few seconds later she said, "Wait a sec, my other line." When she came back she told me it was Tommy, he was stuck at the airport in Boston, "all snowed in." *Snowed-in in Boston?* I remember thinking. *Here I am in Winnipeg, and there's no snow here!* (With one hand Tom is holding the phone to Ruth; with the other hand he is holding onto Greta's, who stands next to him, smirking and sophisticated, in a cool silk suit the colour of cantaloupe. His lover, his teacher in the ways of the world. Tom doesn't let her laugh at Ruth; but they agree, smiling at each other, that Ruth is Good. A Very Good Girl. "Not like you," he says to Greta, desire thickening his voice, and suddenly he is kissing her neck behind the ear, where it is warm and fragrant from her hair. Greta is not good; Greta is powerful.)

"No," says Tom to Ruth when he finally gets home and she offers him some hot chocolate. An egg. A little something. He's already eaten; but more than that he knows that if he says yes, she will sit across from him, and look at him affectionately, admiringly, adoringly: her lord, her darling lord. And he will have to find some way, some pretext, for eating his scrambled egg and his roll and his tomato without looking back at her. Without too obviously rejecting her, without showing how bored he is with her sweet simplicity, how she annoys him with her adulation.

"Thanks anyway," he says, and goes upstairs. Ruth nods understandingly, and with slow sadness, puts away the food.

⋯⊷◉⊶⋯

I can see how it happened the very first time. I can see how it all started. Tom and Greta were together on a North American tour with the Winnipeg symphony, showcasing his first oratorio, *The Voyage of Hope*. Everyone was staying at the same hotel, and one day, walking out together from the group breakfast in the lobby, Greta told Tom that she had to stop by her room for a moment before going to rehearsal, she had forgotten her score. He agreed to accompany her so they could continue what they were talking about. They reached her room, and stepped inside, and suddenly somehow her arms were around him, and his were around her, and they were kissing. Then he, shocked and moral, pulled back, his pallor even paler than before.

But she like a mother soothed him. "Ssh sshh," and she stroked his cheek. And then with affection, (but also mocking him, the way he hated to be mocked) she whispered, "You really *are* a good Catholic boy, aren't you?"

He had spent the whole previous year collaborating with her husband Pietr, the celebrated poet, setting Pietr's allegorical prose poem, *The Voyage of Hope,* into an oratorio. Collaborating with

Pietr sent Tom's career soaring, it propelled him and his work into the public view like a new bird visible for the first time in the sky. Pietr was gracious, too, giving Tom top billing whenever the work appeared, and when he was interviewed for the newspaper or the radio, he spoke with unreserved enthusiasm about Tom and his talent. Greta loved seeing them together: her husband and this young man, awkward, shy, and intense, so like the son she imagined she might have had if she had ever had children. For a year she hovered nearby as the two of them worked at the dining room table. Sometimes she joined them, folding her legs under her on the dining room chair and just listening to them, chin in hand. Then she'd rise, and serve them big mugs of tea. Tom liked his with lots of milk (*like a child*, she thought) and she bought milk just for him, they didn't usually keep it in the house. On two or three occasions, when they were working late and looking quite grey, she cooed and clucked them into taking a break. She unplucked them from the hole they were trapped in, the black hole of creation, and deposited them into the clearer, simpler air of a pretty meal: a cheese soufflé with pink and yellow nasturtiums on the top, and fresh warm bread, and leafy salad with a lemony vinaigrette. Then like good boys they drank their warm tea, and got back to work refreshed and smiling. Greta beamed after one such meal when she overheard Pietr say to Tom, as the two of them walked off toward the study, "Tom, I am one lucky man."

And now, alone with Tom at last, Greta took him into her arms as if comforting him, and began to teach him how to be a man, how to be a man with her. She could feel his surprise at things that, ten years his senior, she took for granted: for instance taking his tongue into her mouth and sucking it slowly in and out many times. He gave a kind of sob and pulled her tight against him, his hand on one of her buttocks; but he almost didn't know what to do after that. She had to help him, touching him here, and there, and even taking his hand and moving it for him when he became paralyzed (with fear? with pleasure? with the pull between right and wrong?). But then after that everything happened very quickly, and suddenly it was over, and he was embarrassed and afraid, but also he wanted her again, and he was ashamed also of that; and she ran her fingers down his cheek, again soothing him:

"It's all right. It's all right, sweet boy."

"I'm not a sweet boy," he growled, and like a boy responding to a dare, climbed on top of her. This time, emboldened, he took her by surprise with his passion and his fierceness, and made her cry out, over and over, her cries growing steadily louder. After that there was no embarrassment between them, they were free with each other and didn't hold anything back. They didn't restrain themselves in public either—although for the first two days Tom was mortified about being seen together, and in anguished tones begged Greta for propriety and caution. But she just laughed at him, ridiculing with witty ruthlessness his bourgeois morality as well as the hypocrisy of those who would presume to judge them. Then she ran her finger along his lip and spoke of the imperatives of love. Soon they were eating their breakfast at a table for two, separate from the others, right in the middle of the lobby; whispering together during the breaks at rehearsals; and disappearing for dinner to restaurants outside the hotel, sitting fearlessly, shamelessly in front of the window, where any passer-by could see them eating and holding hands, clinking and drinking their glasses of wine.

----◦===◦----

The kitchen is filling up now with early-morning sunlight, pale but insistent through white eyelet curtains. The clock says five

after eight: time to start my day, my last day here, I fly this afternoon at five. A great, sweet sadness fills me: *How fleeting the whole
thing is.* My dear Auntie Phaedra, her life as dark and chilly as a
wine cellar filled with unopened bottles. And all of a sudden nothing is real to me, nothing really real except death, and the terrible
loneliness of humans: two people in the dark reaching out for each
other. They want to be naked together, they want to cling to each
other, that's all that they want—and what's so terrible about that?
Soon enough they will be nothing but dust, their bones dissolved
into fine pale powder: they can be as righteous and moral as they
want six feet below the ground. A little warmth in this world, a little comfort and love—a human being deserves it.

I think of Henry and there is a craving in me, a longing and a
loneliness in my body so intense and vivid that it is like a physical pain. I rise abruptly as if, like a cramp in the leg, you can shake
it off by changing positions, you can—if you force yourself to
stand up and walk—scare it away. I make my way over to the sink,
and deposit on its once-white, now rust-stained bottom my
empty coffee cup, pale blue with a thin brown crack down the
side.

Go up, I tell myself. *Go upstairs and try and see Tom and Greta
again in your bed. There is love there. Or if not love, at least some tenderness.*

"Good," says my aunt, as I start up the stairs. "You're coming
off your high horse a bit. Welcome to the human race."

I run the rest of the way, but when I get to the bedroom, all I
can see is the empty bed. I begin to rush around madly, trying to
get dressed, as though it matters what I wear, as though I have
anything to rush to, as if it will make any difference at all what I
do between now and 5:00. I stand in front of my aunt's full-
length, hand-carved mirror, trying on all kinds of clothes: one

~

III

after another I put them on, look in the mirror, rip them off and hurl them onto the floor. Nothing feels right. I become frantic, trying on three, four garments a minute: I couldn't be moving faster if I were running from death itself.

"Slow down," says my aunt. "What are you rushing for?" But I don't have to listen to her any more. She's dead, the ultimate failure after all, so she couldn't have been right about everything. I turn my back on her and her mirror, and without looking at what I'm wearing, I run out of the house.

Outside it is a cool spring day, and everything smells damp and fertile from last night's rain. For a moment I stand at the end of my aunt's walkway where it almost meets the sidewalk. There is perfect visibility today: without squinting I can see clearly all the way down to the river. I begin walking towards it without thinking about where I am going, and within minutes I find myself in a park.

My park. The one I played in almost every day of my child-hood: where I learned to swing myself high on the swings, where I first saw a chipmunk chomp on a nut. Everything looks exactly the same as it used to: the winding path, the patches of sky between the tops of the trees, the mottled shade under the maples. Walking over toward the swings and the slides, I retrace my childhood steps, where I walked not only with my parents, but with all of them: my grandparents, my uncles and my aunts, all my ghosts. Even Henry flashes past me as he was back then, a young man full of dash and promise. Then out of nowhere I hear music. Surprised, I look around for it in the deserted park, and find it on a spruce tree, coming out of a loudspeaker. Now I recall seeing in yesterday's paper that, as part of an educational program ("Sundays in the Park") sponsored by the municipality, they now play "light classical" music here every Sunday between nine and six. I listen for a moment and smile: Mozart's *Requiem*. Someone must have told them Mozart was "light."

I continue my walk feeling jaunty, almost happy, even though I have gone nearly a whole night without sleep. A blue brook runs through the park, and as I cross over it on the little foot-bridge, it gurgles and skips underneath me. I think with pride, as one might think about one's own child, *I am growing up.* It may have taken me longer than everybody else, but now, finally, I understand what others have known for years. That life is short. That if you're lucky enough to find a little warmth, or love, or kindness, you've got to be crazy to pass it by. Seize it with both hands, because this moment will never come again. I look up and see Henry's face smiling at me in the leaves of a tree. Suddenly, terribly, I want to see him again. Maybe we can meet one more time before I fly. We could go for lunch, and then a walk; maybe we will stop walking, and under a tree he will kiss me...

Suddenly this park, although it is the same as it always was, is no longer mine: it belongs only to the past, and I will not be returning to this place. Instantly I feel as light and free as a ghost. I can do anything I want: anything is possible now. Like a visitor from another world, I float invisibly through the park, which is just now starting to fill up with people. I observe them with detachment as they pass me: the miserable-looking couples, with the men and women looking in opposite directions like scales played in counterpoint; the runners in their neon-coloured track suits (running running running from what?); and the slow-walking loners, their faces dazed with loneliness. *The human condition.* Once again I hear the somber, funereal tones of the *Requiem* emanating from a tree. *Is there not one—one single couple in this whole park joyfully making love on the grass?* Just then I see a woman waving toward me with a stiff-fingered wave. I try to ignore her—of course she can't be waving at me—but she keeps on smiling and waving more and more energetically, as she and someone with her draw nearer. I look behind me, there is no one there, she must be waving at me. But I can't understand how she can be: how can she even see me, if I'm a ghost? And how can she possibly know me? I don't know anyone here. Then the woman stands several feet in front of me, still smiling, with a girl by her side, and I see who it is.

It's Ruth.

Her eyes, looking at me, are the same startling ochre they always were; her hair is still dark, though longer than I remember it; and her bearing, as usual, regal yet friendly. I recognize the eyes, the hair, the way of carrying herself, even the style of dress in her high-waisted flowered frock. After all, I have seen her every few years. A person doesn't change overnight. Yet I feel that I am looking at a stranger, someone I don't know, as she flutters her hands at me in nervous greeting.

She is with a girl of about eleven: this must be Rebecca, her oldest. Ruth's arm is clamped around the girl, and she squeezes her tightly to her every ten seconds or so in a convulsive gesture of which she seems unaware. The girl has her father's eyes—pale grey in very deep sockets—and Ruth's heart-shaped lips. Not pretty, but she has that stamp on her: of blessing, of love. For no logical reason my heart begins to pound, as if with guilt. But what have I done? Thought about Ruth? Thought about her husband, and pictured him in bed with his lover? Been silent, complicit, by not phoning her up last night as soon as I heard, and telling her what I know?

Of course I've done nothing. But anyway my smile feels forced as I greet her:

"Ruth! What are you doing here?"

"Oh, just going for a walk. We like to do that, eh, Rebecca?" she says, turning to the girl. "You know who this lady is? She used to be my babysitter! Just like you have Bernadette..."

That is unfair, and ghost or no ghost, that hurts. As though that is all that I am, all that I ever was, to her. She, whom I've worried about, on whose behalf I've hated her husband and been angry at total strangers. She, who in a crucial moment came between me and Henry, my lover-to-be.

She doesn't ask what I'm doing in town, or how long I'm staying. She just chatters on and on about herself, intermittently clutching the girl in a gesture that is affectionate, but also anguished like the wringing of hands. She doesn't linger long, she doesn't invite me home with them for brunch, which is where she says they have to rush off to. But that's okay; something about her makes me tremble inside, makes me want to get away from her as fast as possible. Maybe it's her laugh, which is no longer the one I remember, but more like her mother's now: phony-sounding and shrill, on the edge of losing control, like a singer sliding out of her range. But also it's the way she talks and talks about herself, as though I have been put on this earth solely to be her audience: to be her witness, to bear witness to her and her life. And the way she looks away when she laughs—where is she looking? Who is she looking to? To the mountains, whence cometh her help? There is nothing near us but the old brick building which now houses the toilets of the park—and where once, long ago, I lined up with the other children in front of the northern wall, and through an open window in the brick, bought French fries and ice cream cones with nickels sweaty from my palm.

I know suddenly, and with absolute certainty, that Ruth knows about Tom and Greta. I can feel it: her core is gone, her insides are hollow—like a tin soldier that keeps on marching because someone once wound it up, but resounding through its every movement is the echo of hollow tin. Ruth goes on chattering away charmingly, meaninglessly, gesturing stiffly with her one free hand. I watch her perform, and I feel the way you feel when you see a shattered bird lying in the middle of the street. Someone's run over it. There's nothing you can do. But anyway (although you know it's pointless, and even a little bit foolish) you sometimes get out of your car and go over and take a look. You stand for a moment in silence and watch it. You admire the final fluttering of its wings.

Yosepha

AROUND HER MOTHER'S swollen belly swarmed her many half brothers and sisters: All sizes and shapes, they laid their hands fearfully upon her belly, or pressed their ears to it to try and hear the life within. Rachel, an intense and private woman, was so transformed at the thought of having a child of her own, that initially she only laughed at the wonder and worry of her stepchildren, and let them lay their hands upon her.

But Rachel was a woman of many fears and dreams; and later on in the pregnancy, curled beside her husband at night, she confided her fears to him in a whisper. She told him that his children had organized against her —they all hated her baby, they wanted it to die. In many small incidents she found evidence of this: they had brought her dirty water to drink, they had pinched her stomach instead of stroking it, and lately they murmured among themselves and fell silent when she approached. At night she wept, What if they hated her baby? What if she died in childbirth, and she couldn't protect it from them? *He* would have to protect their baby...Yaacov just kissed her temple, and stroked her hair, and even though this made her smile, a little darkness still remained in her eyes. "Do you doubt me, Rachel?" he asked her. "With all my love for you, and you doubt me?" Then the darkness vanished from her eyes, seeping somewhere inside where he couldn't see it any more, and—helpless against these fears of hers, these dreams and superstitions in which her family believed—Yaacov did the only thing he knew. He took her in his arms, wrapping her in his love, like a cloak.

For five years they had been waiting for this. For five years they'd been tending sheep on their *moshav* in southern Israel, reading and rereading the works of Herzl, Gordon, and Ahad Ha'am, and rejoicing—as one did in the early years of the State—in the honour of fulfilling the Zionist dream. But through all this, they had also been waiting. And now, with both of them past their prime, they were eager and impatient for this child. True, Yaacov already had six sons; but he did not yet have the son he wanted. With each son born, he had looked into the infant's eyes, and wondered, *Is this the one?* Would this be the one who had appeared to him in his dreams—the great leader of his people who would carry the Zionist hope forward into the next generation, and deliver them all from untold dangers and disasters? Yaacov envisioned for his people a great future, as expansive as the sea, with descendants and generations as many as the fish that fill it. And yet, with each son, he could see that this was not the one he'd been promised, the one to fulfill this destiny. Rachel knew his disappointment and secretly rejoiced. His first wife may have given him twelve children, spawned like so many fish; but *hers* would bear the star on his forehead. *My son*, she thought, *it will be* my *son...*

And the child-to-be, the prince—the comfort of their old age and the leader of his people—reached the time of his birth.

⤙══◎═⤏

At the time of its birth, the baby lay dying. When they smashed open the womb, it began to die, all around it scattered its life, its hope, the remnants of its world. It watched the broken pieces of womb and the liquid—the warm globulating stuff that had held it so secure—go cold, dry up, in this new air. In an eternity of waiting, it had prepared itself for this instant. In the months of rocking wombness, it had planned for this moment when it would emerge, show itself to its creator, and be saved from the death in this new world. The midwife's hands were soft and skillful, but the baby knew that she wasn't its mother: It would not open its eyes to her. It held itself back, fists clenched tight, until it smelled a certain smell, sensed a certain sense that said: *Mother*. The being in it, the being of its being, began to unfold. Slowly, luxuriously it opened, and its eyes opened, and it presented itself defenselessly to its mother.

"A girl," urged the wholesome midwife. "A daughter..."

For only one moment, only a fraction of a moment, Rachel looked at, and appraised, the naked being before her. Looked at, and appraised. And her lids snapped shut against her like two steel doors.

The midwife swept away, rocked against her breast, the screaming, terrified infant. "Now now, now now," she clucked as she rocked her. "Now now. Now now." Everyone, even the shepherds miles away, could hear the baby screaming in the midwife's hut well into the night. Nothing could comfort her. To the other women in the hut, the midwife, jiggling the baby, expressed her disapproval. "Can you imagine?" she said. "And such a pretty baby, too."

But no one spread the story around, and it never turned into gossip. For Rachel, that very night, from some unnamed inner bleeding, died.

⊷═◯═⊷

Yaacov never quite recovered. He retired, under some pretense or other, from public affairs. He spent more and more time alone in his work tent ("thinking," he said), and emerged only occasionally—holding his clipboard with a pencil attached by a string—to look over his sheep. Whatever he was told by his assistant, the young man who had come to help him from a neighbouring *moshav*, whatever figures or reports he was given, he nodded his head vaguely like one who's lost his sight, saying, "I see, I see," or "Yes, of course," as if he were stupid not to already have known. The eyes of his assistant grew shrewder and shrewder, and as time went on, his profits began dwindling, sheep began to get lost, and there were always excuses...

The man was suddenly old.

His children grew up around him, barefoot with their lower legs suntanned and dusty from playing jumping games outdoors and from herding sheep. The boys were back-slapping, hearty farmer's boys, which surprised him, despite the fact that this was what he had raised them to be. Like the rest of his generation, Yaacov had decried the pasty-faced scholars of the *shtetl*, and dreamed of "the new Jew"—a Whole Man, who would live not only by his mind, but by his hands, as well—and who, by the work of his hands, would redeem The Land. Yet the mind and the soul that Yaacov had taken for granted were not in his sons, and this struck horror into his heart. His girls, too, were strangers to him. They cackled in front of mirrors, grabbing ribbons from each other, and playing women games that he didn't understand, and all he could do was take himself away from them with a philosophical gaze, having patted one or another of them vaguely on the head. The boys, like animals, were always engrouped, and so were the girls—they huddled together, boys on one side, girls on the other, near the entrance to his tent—and so Yaacov began confusing their names. They all looked alike to him anyway, the six girls in their clothes that flapped at him like flags, and the six boys with their demands and wants and affections that came and went with the wind.

Yet he had a place for Yosepha, his skinny-legged daughter who was pale-faced and solitary as Rachel had been, and whose black eyes, with all their intensity, had answered his silent question, *Yes* before he'd asked. In the fading clarity of his mind, he thought of her neither as a girl nor a boy, but as something in-between. Rachel had said, before the birth, that she wanted the child to be called Yoseph, and out of respect for her memory, Yaacov had kept this name. He had added the requisite suffix "a," of course, to put it into the feminine form; but sometimes he forgot the "a", and just called her Yoseph instead. And Yosepha didn't seem to mind. She somehow seemed to understand, even without being told, the expectation and disappointment behind her name, and answered to both Yoseph and Yosepha. Yaacov confused other things, too, like Rachel's death and Yosepha's birth. These two things became utterly fused in his mind, so that after a while, Yosepha and Rachel no longer seemed to him like separate entities, but just two different bodies containing the same passionate soul. Like two different vessels carrying the same wine.

>⇒◎⟨<

But this is not why she was his chosen one. If you had asked Yaacov what was special about Yosepha—why it was her, and not any of his other children—he would have spoken to you not of her soul, but of her mind. She had an eerie way of seeing right through to the essence of a thing—of a problem, or a person—in an instant separating wheat from chaff, and slicing through to the core. She did not know she was doing this. For her it was instinctive, like a rat impatiently avoiding the false leads in a maze, and going straight for the cheese. Yosepha's mind strained forward like that, toward the essence of things, as if she had no time, as if her life depended on it.

Dresses and chatter filled her with horror.

Even when she was a young child, her brothers stuck out their lower lips and frowned when she spoke, as over and over she seemed to hit, with no effort at all, exactly the answer that Yaacov was waiting for. As Yosepha grew older, she and Yaacov would sometimes engage, during the midday meal, in heady dialogues that left her brothers and sisters picking at their food and exchanging looks. Yosepha loved to read, and would recite to Yaacov from whatever she was reading—from the poet Rachel, or from Gordon on the idea of the redemption of The Land. Occasionally, too, she would tell him about something she'd read in the local agricultural bulletin, on crop rotation for example, or the latest developments in sheep farming. Once after reading there about the need for new, more modern methods, Yosepha said at the dinner table that she wanted to do something important with her life, she wanted to *contribute* somehow. She dreamed of maybe starting up a collective of all the sheep farms in the region, helping to lead them toward mechanization and modernization. Or maybe she could work with Krause and others like him who were trying to revolutionize agriculture at the national level, encouraging more scientific knowledge and technological innovation, and increasing the country's hydroelectric power. Maybe she could help them do it—help them bring about the necessary changes—so that in the coming years, Israel could compete in the regional markets (maybe even the world markets, later on). Her brothers and sisters stared at her, and then rolled their eyes at each other.

"Why aim so low?" Shimon sneered at her from across the table. "Why not become our Prime Minister, when Ben-Gurion's done his term? Or better yet, why not leader of the world?"

"Sssh, ssssh," hushed Yaacov; but to Yosepha he said, "One shouldn't speak that way. You invite ridicule and the anger of others by being boastful. Such dreams are best kept to yourself."

❖══◎══❖

Yosepha's brothers tried to please Yaacov the only way they knew how: by giving him gifts. They did this individually, each of them plotting alone, and sneaking into Yaacov's tent when they thought no one else was looking. For although the brothers were close, as close as brothers can be, for this they sparred separately, each willingly betraying the other. One at a time they stood before Yaacov in uncomplicated worship, longing only to serve and be loved; and stretching forth their hands, they laid their gifts—gifts of wood or cloth or stone, laboured over with love—on the table near their father. Yaacov received these offerings absent-mindedly, with vague "thank you"s. He was not an unkind man, he never pushed them away; but neither did he draw them nearer. The son's disappointment and mystification, once outside the tent, turned to rage, but it was quickly swallowed and kept from the others. Stealthily, and with shame, each one rejoined the group, smoldering hate within his heart and a longing for revenge. Each of them remembered, like a myth repolished, the position of his gift on Yaacov's table, and knew that there it would sit, unstroked and uncherished, in the days to come.

The sisters vied for Yaacov's affection by trying to impress him with their beauty. They showed off their new dresses, posing this way and that, they flashed at him their various-coloured eyes, and tried to stand as close to him as they could. Each of them secretly hoped that he would rest his eyes on her, stroke her cheek, and say how pretty she'd become; but he never did. He bumbled his way back to his tent, leaving behind him a burning hum, not unlike a swarm of bees, each one longing to be queen.

Yosepha's brothers and sisters were all united by their unshared wounds, as families are often most deeply united through their secrets, and not through what is openly shared. Each of the brothers and sisters was blood of Yaacov's blood, and flesh of Yaacov's flesh.

⊷━◉═◉━⊷

Late one afternoon, when the wind was blowing and the sand flew up into the eyes and the mouth, the brothers huddled together as usual on one side of the entrance to Yaacov's tent, and the sisters huddled on the other. They were busy with their separate occupations: the brothers playing knives, becoming men; and the sisters playing primp and preen, becoming women. And around both groups, whirls of dust.

Yosepha was alone, partway between the two groups —slightly closer to her sisters, but a safe distance from them, too. She was further than all the others from the door of her father's tent, but was facing it as she knelt on a flat rock, reading a book —or trying to look as if she were reading. With each wave of laughter from her sisters, she narrowed her eyes more intensely, as if fighting off loneliness, as if telling herself: *I don't need them.* She bit her lips, and they got redder as she read.

The flap to Yaacov's tent flew open. The wind blew hard and some birds squawked in the late autumn sky. His sons and daughters stopped what they were doing, and grew silent and still, as he stood squarely, framed by the entrance to his tent.

He stood a few moments, just listening to the air and breathing it in. Then he said, "Yosepha. Where is Yosepha?"

She leapt to her feet. "Here, father!" she cried tremulously.

"Come here," he said.

She walked to him eagerly, aware of being watched, aware of the gloomy and ominous packs to her left and right: one heavy and male, like cattle, the other lighter but sharper, like pecking birds. She felt their collective hatred like a force, and her knees trembled a little as she walked between them.

When she reached Yaacov she stood before him, and he put his right hand gently on her head. He squinted first at the brothers, then at the sisters, and they watched him, their furry-haired father with his hand on Yosepha's head. She was seventeen by now, but she still looked as slender as a boy, and totally untouched by the sun that had burnt them all brown. With his left hand, Yaacov reached inside his coat, drew from it a small, beautifully bound book, and handed it to Yosepha. She looked down at it for a moment, and then stared with wonder at Yaacov.

"Your copy of Herzl," she said. "The one you brought with you from Russia."

Her father nodded. "'If you will it, it is no dream.' Do great things, Yosepha," he said. "Listen to those dreams of yours." He stood for another moment, smiling down at her. Then he took his hand from her head, and without looking at his other children, turned on his heel like a monarch, and re-entered his tent. The tent-flap dropped behind him like a slap.

Holding the book on her head with her right hand, Yosepha sauntered her way back, between brothers and sisters, to her place on the rock. The book looked like a crown in the sun.

2.

Twenty-two years passed. Twenty-two years since the day that Yaacov had publicly isolated and blessed his daughter. And twenty-two years less a week since Yosepha's brothers and sisters took her with them on a trip to the Negev, and abandoned her on the way home, on a dark road at nightfall. The Negev was a full day's drive from their *moshav*, and totally unpopulated except for some Bedouins from whom, every year at this time, they bought some new sheep. By the end of the second day, they'd concluded all their business and begun the trip home; but after they'd been driving for about an hour, the truck suddenly stopped, and her brothers and sisters told Yosepha to get out and walk the rest of the way. She sat there, confused, thinking they were joking; and then they grabbed her and pushed her off the back of the truck, and pried her fingers loose when she clung to it—and afterwards again when she ran after them and caught up to the truck and tried to climb back on. They laughed at her, taunting her as they drove off: "'Do great things, Yosepha!' Don't worry! Your daddy will come and save you!" Twenty-two years since Yosepha had learned what it was to be truly alone in the world, to rely upon people where necessary, but never to trust them; and to try and carve for herself whatever shape of a life her gifts and fortunes permitted her.

She spent two nights and two days alone by the side of that road, sitting, lying down, or walking, hoping that sooner or later someone would pass by—a caravan of Bedouins maybe—and pick her up. She was terrified that whole first night, trying to sleep, freezing, and alone, in a ditch; and no less frightened all the next day in the brutal heat in the middle of nowhere, without food or water. At twilight, after two days, she was so parched and hungry, cold and exhausted, that when she saw a small jeep in the distance coming up the road, she thought she was seeing a mirage. In it were a man and a woman, kibbutzniks, it turned out, from a kibbutz far up north near the Lebanese border. The woman told Yosepha that they were building the very first kibbutz in that part of the country: They and eight other pioneers ("Crazy people may be more like it," the man laughed) had started it only five and a half months before. They already had tents up, and facilities for washing and cooking, a few chickens, and the beginnings of a garden. They had to manage their water very carefully, but they were getting by. The woman gave Yosepha a drink from her canteen, and some bread, and said that she was welcome to join them, if she liked. *And why not?* thought Yosepha. She had no way to get home fraom where she was, and this kibbutz sounded no worse than any place else. She'd stay for a while, and make her brothers and sisters worry—they'd have to come looking for her, they'd have to climb the whole height of this country to find her. Let them have a scare. Let them think that maybe she was dead. Yosepha told the woman and the man that she'd come for a while and see. Then she fell asleep in the back seat of the jeep, being bounced over the bumpy roads like a sack of flour, or a corpse.

The kibbutz was nothing but some tents erected on an ancient hill. It was nothing but a dream. But to Yosepha it seemed fine. And when the days turned into weeks, and the weeks into months, and there was no sign of her father, or her sisters or brothers, looking for her, she thought, *To hell with them. What should I go back for?* It would be a long and difficult journey—five or six days at least—to get back home. Public transportation was almost non-existent then—there were barely even roads yet—and of course the kibbutz couldn't lend her either its jeep or its truck for such a long time. It would mean hitching rides all the way back, once again waiting nights and days by the side of the road. *Forget it*, she decided. *If they don't care, I don't care.* She threw herself into her work on the kibbutz, and for being such a dedicated worker, she quickly won the kibbutzniks' respect. At first she did the same things as everybody else: building wooden shacks, clearing away stones, and planting a vegetable garden. But after a while they noticed that she had the wondrous ability to make anything grow, anywhere she wanted. Sometimes she dreamed it the night before, in one of her strange, multi-coloured dreams: *This plant—here, in this corner. That one—over there, by the tree.* The next day she'd plant them, against all logic, and they would grow exactly as she'd dreamed. The kibbutz encouraged her to experiment, they gave her a free hand—and her successes were so unexpected, and dramatic, so unlike what anyone else was able to accomplish at that time, that within months she had caught the attention of the government. To the Ministry of Agriculture, she was a dream come true, the land being, as it was, rocky, stubborn, and for the most part unarable. Yosepha could grow things practically in rock. She grew bright, burning poppies on an all but waterless diet; bougainvillea in desert chalk, fruit trees in weak, tired earth. There seemed to be nothing she couldn't do. The Ministry was also thirsty for a solution to the problem of Israel's water shortage, and Yosepha had exciting new ideas. By the time she had been away from home for seventeen years, she had more than half the kibbutzim in the north irrigating with her method; five years after that, she was made Assistant Deputy Minister of Agriculture; and several weeks later, consonant with one of her most vivid and disturbing dreams, drought struck the land.

The drought struck hard, and nowhere so hard as in the South where, unbeknownst to Yosepha, her father's sheep grew thin and

128

keeled over, one by one. The "crisis in the South," as it came to be called, occupied Yosepha's thoughts night and day, though it had nothing to do with her being from there, or her family. She actually remembered very little of her home or her father, other than the warmth of his body when he touched her on the head or stood near her, and the dank, sharp odour of his sheepskin tent. During the first months on the kibbutz, when he hadn't come looking for her, when it seemed that he didn't care whether she lived or died, she discovered in herself a bitterness towards him so deep that it all but eclipsed her hatred for her brothers and sisters. As time went on, she thought about them all less and less, and threw herself into her new surroundings as thoroughly as she had wiped out the old. She retained, however, a horror for dryness and dust, and a fascination with water; and these elements, though never thought about, were deep in her, and moved her through her search to irrigate with a kind of irresistible force, an almost flawless intuition.

She began to dream nightly of saving the South: watering it with one gigantic sprinkler, arching water over its parched fields like a rainbow. She dreamed of bringing the life back into the land, making it burst into bloom with new and unheard-of flowers, and colouring the desert purple and red. She infected the Prime Minister with her dream, and funds for this project poured her way. He said to her, "I will establish an institute in the South, and you will teach the farmers there to irrigate. You will fill all our deserts with life."

They flowed from all over to Yosepha's institute: herdsmen, farmers, kibbutzniks, and shepherds, all of them with that struck, panicked look in the eye of men who have watched their sheep, cattle, or fieldcrops die—and thought, as baldly as this: *I could die, too*. Nothing less than mad desperation would have brought these men to seek help from a woman—especially one like her, as slight as a girl, pale, and unmarried.

They came to Yosepha in droves, and sat at her feet.

One day in late August, when Yosepha was just finishing her daily inspection of the Institute and preparing to lock up and go home, a man approached her. To Yosepha he looked like all the others, crude and hairy, although also handsome in a way with his rough good looks.

"Are you the director?" he asked her.

"I am."

"I beg of you to help us."

Like countless times before, Yosepha asked the man where he was from (the South, of course), what kind of a *moshav* he had, how large it was, and so on. Only after he'd told his story did she ask more personal questions. The exact location of the *moshav*? The age of the father? The number of children? And then, the name.

On seeing before her her brother Shimon, Yosepha's first reaction was an almost physical revulsion. *So this was it: This hairy being in need was now bowing before her—this being, how dare he live!* Rushing back at Yosepha like water came the terror she had felt by the side of the road, the cold, the terror, the hunger. The fear, the hatred. The fear. And Yosepha excused herself.

When she returned, she said to him, "We are very busy here, as you must realize, and very short-staffed. There is no point in teaching you alone. According to our policy, it is necessary for all those involved in our project to understand the underlying principles. Go home, and bring back with you every member of your family—all your brothers and sisters, and your father, as well. Then we can help you."

Shimon protested: His father was too old, there was too much work to be done at home, no way could everyone be spared at once. Yosepha shrugged. "I'm sorry, then," she said.

Not until several months later did Shimon return. From her window, Yosepha watched the arrival of the big, dust-covered jeep as it rattled its way up to the entrance of the Institute. Out of the jeep tumbled a man and a woman, then another man and another woman, all of them dark and dusty from the journey. Yosepha recognized them, and had to turn away.

"Give me a few minutes," she said to her secretary, "before bringing in this new group. And make some tea, please—mint is what they like."

It was starting to come back to her. She stood behind the desk in her office as if it were a shield, and buried her face in her hands.

My God! What should I do? What can I say to them? And then: *Can I ever forgive...?*

It had cost her not to, and she knew it. It had cost her to wipe out their memory but nurture the hatred, preserve and feed her seething, nameless anger. She had hated her brothers and sisters, but she had also hated herself, she had hated being small and afraid on that road. And she hated her father, too. It was his love, after all, that had spawned their hatred; their hatred was as natural as bacteria feeding on milk in the sun. No, she could not forgive him for cursing her as he had with his blessing. She would not release the past, she would not betray the girl that she had been...

Her secretary knocked, motioned the visitors in ahead of her, then followed with a tray of tea which she set on Yosepha's desk. "That will be all," Yosepha said to her, and she left. Yosepha counted the glasses of tea: fourteen. Fourteen Duralex glasses, huddled together on the tray, like a family. No one glass could be moved without touching another.

Glancing up for only an instant, Yosepha said, "Help yourselves to tea, and have a seat," and she herself took a glass, and began drinking, still on her feet. She looked at the irrigation map on the wall to her left, and not at her visitors, as they came forward to take their tea, and sat down on the sofas in her office, sipping. They sat and she stood. The sun shone in from the window behind her, and touched the top of her head. She put down her glass, and looked up.

Their eyes were watching her, every pair of eyes, and as Yosepha gazed into them, one after another, she felt herself weaken. For strength, she looked away from them to the far corner of the room, and there, suddenly, she saw her old father.

My God, she thought. *How you've aged!*

She stared at him. Then at her brothers and sisters, one by one. She couldn't speak. She just looked at them and tears ran down her face. They stared at her, astonished. Gesturing with one hand, she said, as if in explanation,

"I am Yosepha."

Her brothers and sisters all looked at each other, frightened; but not one of them said a word. At the back of the room the old man rose from his chair.

"Yosepha," he said. "Alive?! Is it possible? Is it *you?*"

Yosepha looked at his face. *He didn't know,* she thought. *He never knew what really happened.* She'd thought he *did,* she'd assumed he knew and just didn't care. He must have thought...all these years...They must have told him...

Never mind. It doesn't matter now.

Yosepha looked at her brothers and sisters, seated before her with bowed heads. "Don't be afraid," she said. "The past has passed. I will restore the life to your land and your flocks, and you will be rich and prosper. I will take care of you—you are my family."

And then she went over to Yaacov, staring toward her voice as though listening to a dream. She put her hands on his cheeks. And from a place so deep in her, she herself was surprised, she said to him:

"You I forgive."

Flesh

Part One

I have a cousin who hasn't left the house in twenty years. Well, that's not quite true—once a year she walks with her mother next door to Auntie Dorothy's, to the other half of the semi-detached house, and sits for a half-hour with the two old ladies in the living room that is a replica of her own, except that everything is laid out exactly backwards. This annual ritual happens every February when Auntie Bella and Auntie Dorothy are about to go off alone together for a week to Florida, leaving behind them two identical freezers full of food, one for my cousin Pearl, and one for a disgruntled Uncle Herb. Other than this, Pearl never leaves the

~

house. She doesn't look like what you'd think of as a hermit (someone dressed in foul-smelling rags, with a long grey beard); she is unusually thin and pale, but other than this appears quite normal. Psychiatrists, psychologists, social workers—no one has been able to figure it out. In the first few years, Auntie Bella dragged a string of professionals to the house, paying them exorbitant fees with money that she didn't have, because even then, no one did "house calls" any more. One after another, they sat on the old, green living room couch, their hands dangling between their knees, while Auntie Bella stood outside Pearl's door, banging on it, begging her to come out and talk to "the nice man who's only here to help." She hasn't done this for at least fifteen years, though, since the last one left shaking his head and Pearl threatened to kill herself if Auntie Bella ever tried this again. The two of them have lived in quiet isolation ever since, with Pearl passing her days silently in her room, and Auntie Bella cooking, cleaning, and clay-sculpting (three-inch figurines, the size of her index finger), every day till 1:30, when she goes next door to Auntie Dorothy's for the afternoon. Evenings end early, watching T.V.

We were friends once, Pearl and I—best friends. It makes you feel weird, in a way, having been best friends with someone who is now a loonie tune, a loser, a wipe-out. You can't help asking yourself if there isn't something a little bit wrong with you too, for having loved somebody like that. Like later in college when I picked up this guy at a party, and under the dim lights and the warm touch of his hand, everything felt right, and we left the party early to go back to his place. But the next morning, when I looked at him in the light of day, I was appalled, and ashamed of the need that had made him seem okay.

Pearl and I were close once, I won't deny it. I lived only two doors down from her, on the other side of Auntie Dorothy, and we were the only girls in our generation, the only female cousins in a slew of sweaty, smelly, sports-crazed males. On long summer days, Pearl and I used to tie one end of the skipping rope to the door handle of her garage, turn the rope for each other, and skip until the sun slowly went down behind us and it was too dark to skip any more. She was one year older than I, and when I was six, she taught me how to read, playing teacher in front of a little blackboard on an easel in her basement. We argued over the spelling of the word "why." She said it was just a word; but I said no, it was a question—you couldn't have the word "why" without having a question mark after it, because you couldn't have the word "why" without it being a question. She, being the teacher, threw the chalk at me and shrieked that I was so stupid I'd never learn how to read, I'd never even pass grade one. Now I can see she was right in a way: A word is just a word, after all—it's not necessarily always a question. Yet, maybe because it's the first word I ever learned to spell, or because this was the first time Pearl and I ever really fought, it became *my* word, my primary word, the prism through which everything shines for me.

Why? Why? Why? echoes in me all the time.

Two days ago Auntie Bella died. We sit in her living room, surrounded by her things: her framed photographs on the end tables (the most prominent of them being her wedding picture, and a shot of her holding Pearl as a baby); her triple-tiered silver filigree candy dish holding pistachio nuts at the top, then sugar-coated almonds, and below them chocolate-covered mints; and over by the window, her African violets in their seven little pots. She died suddenly of a heart attack. Shocking, even though she was seventy-two, not because "she'd never been sick a day in her life," but on the contrary, because she'd been sick just about every single day of it since she was born. She almost died at birth (she was very premature, and she came out so small and blue that no one expected her to survive); she spent half her childhood and adolescence alone with her mother in the country, trying to clear a spot on the lung; after giving birth to Pearl, she became so ill she had to go to a sanatorium for almost a year; and after *that*, it was always one thing or another. Whenever you'd go to visit her, she'd show you entire shoeboxes full of multicoloured pills, some as brilliant and beautiful as gems, the way other women showed off their jewelry collections. She looked sick, and she talked sick, and you always felt when you visited her that this was it, that you would never see her alive again. But then, of course, she'd be fine, and despite the complaints, and the huge bags under her eyes, and the warnings whispered to us by her doctors, she lived on and on and on. As my dad used to say, "Don't worry about my sister Bella—she'll outlive me, and half our friends, as well." And he was right. She did. We started to think that if there was anyone in the world who was never going to die, it was her. So it was a terrible shock to us all when she did, when she finally really died.

We sit in a circle, sitting *shiva*, and for the first time since the funeral, there is a lull in the constant onslaught of visitors. Mid-afternoon on the second day, and suddenly we are alone together, just the family, without all the neighbours, acquaintances and friends. The purpose of *shiva* is for everyone to comfort "the bereaved"; in this case, according to Jewish law, that means only Auntie Dorothy, the sole surviving sibling, and Pearl. Auntie Dorothy sits on a low chair, as is the custom for mourners, her back straight and her face pale. But the second low chair, the one for Pearl, stands empty. Her absence is terrible, especially now in the sudden stillness, with all the guests gone. It feels like a ghost-*shiva*: How can we comfort if the bereaved are not all here to be comforted? It angers us obscurely, her depriving us of the one thing that might comfort us right now: ritual duty, doing what is expected, giving to the mourners so we can feel we have something to give.

But Pearl wants none of it. Whatever we are selling, she doesn't want to buy. She is upstairs in her room, with the door closed as usual, probably laughing at us, or hating us, just waiting for us to leave. God only knows what she's doing—sitting cross-legged on her bed, I guess, like she used to back then when I was still allowed into her room. I was fifteen to her sixteen the last time she let me in, and I sat facing her on her bed, cross-legged too. We talked about conformity, she warned me against "playing the game," she said I was becoming just like everybody else, did I want to wind up in one of those "boxes on the hillside," like the people in our favourite song? I didn't know what to say. We were already drifting apart, and she told me that if, on Saturday night, I wore the frilly pink blouse and the navy blue "elephant" pants that I'd bought especially for my class party, if I put on the eyeliner and mascara and lipstick and blush-on that I'd bought the day before at the drugstore, then I would be "selling out," and she would be really disappointed in me. I didn't have a big sister, or even any other friends, I really didn't have anyone but Pearl—and losing her respect, losing her, hurt as much as anything else that has happened to me in the twenty-six years since. But I did look beautiful at the party that night. Boys noticed me, and for the first time ever, I got asked to dance. Bobby Zuker and I even danced slow together once, to "Homeward Bound"; and in spite of Pearl, at the end of the evening I let him give me my very first kiss.

Suddenly a loud, guttural voice booms through the room, and all the whispered conversations instantly come to a halt.

"Vot are vee going to do?" bellows my great-aunt Bryna, and everyone gives her their full attention. My father's Auntie Bryna is

~

137

ninety-four and almost blind, but her voice with the strong Russian accent is still as indomitable as it must have been when she was a young girl in the old country, bossing around chickens and cows.

Everyone immediately understands what she's talking about. No one has to ask "Do about what?" because this is the same question that we have all been whispering to each other, and when we haven't been whispering it to each other, we have been whispering it to ourselves: What will happen now to Pearl? Who will look out for her? Who will buy and prepare her food, replace her clothes when they start wearing out? Who will speak to her once in a while, to keep her voice from rusting, to make sure she doesn't forget how to speak?

And of course, underneath these questions, there is another question, the compelling, unspoken, unspeakable one, which is, How did this happen? How did this happen to us? To good people, decent people, normal people? How did we end up with Pearl, who is flawed, defective, a failure of a human being? She started out well enough, just like everybody else, normal physically, and with a normal IQ (more than normal, actually, scoring "very bright" on the IQ test we took in high school). She was nice-looking, too: slim with short dark hair. A sweet, if serious, little girl. Whatever happened to her along the way? Was there something we could have, should have, seen? Something we could have, should have, done? (The others, I think, brush off this last question without too much thought: *What could I have done?* they'd say. *How am I to blame for how Pearl turned out?* But I remember the tricks they played on her, and the teasing, and I know that they are not totally blameless. None of us are. Not even me.)

"She cannot live here alone," declares my Auntie Bryna, and there are nods, and sighs, and a lot of looking down into teacups. All of us cousins have come in from out of town, from Toronto,

Vancouver, Ottawa, Seattle. No one lives in Montreal any more except the older generation. None of us can take this on.

My cousins Howie and Michael make some half-hearted suggestions, and Michael's second wife, a blond from Seattle, chimes in with something about a homemaker. But none of these ideas make any sense for Pearl. There is an uncomfortable silence. Then Auntie Bryna says decisively,

"I think she should go to a group home. I saw on television. A place for all kinds people—idiot people, crazy people, anybody can't live by themself, they can live in this group home."

"It's not a bad idea," says Uncle Herb.

"What?" I cry. "You can't put Pearl in a group home!" I am appalled at my great-aunt's crudeness, and the indifferent acquiescence of my uncle. Pearl is not an idiot or a crazy person. Nor is she a wounded calf, to be left to die at the edge of the herd. I know group homes. As a psychologist-in-training I did my first residency in a group home for young adults. The kids, as we called them, wandered aimlessly around the house, unwashed and uncared for, and the only time they evoked any real response from the staff was when they did something wrong, often out of sheer boredom. The crackdown then was immediate and brutal: Four or five staff members would jump on the offending young person, pinning them down by their arms and legs. Sometimes they hurt the kids, and there were bruises, even injuries, after "restraint," although the staff always claimed they never meant to. A place, I remember, of tyrannical control and conformity.

Everyone is staring at me. My teacup trembles on its saucer. "She'd hate it there," I add lamely.

No one says anything. Auntie Bryna, Auntie Dorothy, and Uncle Herb, the grown-ups, just look at me. They can't afford to dismiss me the way they do my cousins and their wives. I am the only woman in my generation (not counting Pearl, but of course Pearl doesn't count). It is I who will hold the family together, carrying the torch into the next generation, taking over from Auntie Dorothy whose turn it is now. Soon it will be up to me to keep the connections alive, to maintain and—where necessary—mend the web. It is me who everyone will call to find out the address of a second cousin who lives in Greece, because it's always good to have the name of someone you know when you're going to a strange place, and their son is going traveling—and they thought maybe he could look up Jeffrey, cousin Louie's boy, wasn't he teaching English in Mikonos the last anyone heard? It is a role with honour that awaits me, but it is also a weight, like a royal mantle of heavy purple silk pressing on my shoulders even before it's mine.

Auntie Dorothy is looking at me steadily but not unkindly.

"Can you think of any other solution?" she asks.

"I don't know," I say irritably. Then, after a pause: "Has anyone even talked to Pearl? Maybe she has some ideas about what she'd like to do."

Somebody snickers. But Auntie Dorothy looks at me thoughtfully. "Perhaps it's worth a try," she says. "There's certainly nothing to lose...Maybe you, dear, could speak to her, and see what she has to say. She'll listen to you."

Listen to me! This was always Auntie Bella's phrase. "Talk to Pearl," she would plead, "she'll listen to you..." As if I have, as if I ever had, any influence with her at all. When I was in college, Auntie Bella would follow this sentence with "Can't you take her to a party, or a movie, sometime? Just let her go around with you and your friends a bit. Maybe it would draw her out..." After a while she gave up on that, and then for about five years she would follow "Talk to Pearl, she'll listen to you" with "You're good with people. You're a psychologist"— as though that has ever helped anyone with anything.

"I've hardly talked to her since high school," I protest. "She won't even let me into her room."

"Please," says Auntie Dorothy with a rare gentleness. "Please try." And I realize what it must be like for her, to be mourning her last sibling, but also her best friend, someone she has seen, and talked to, every day of her life, except for the two weeks they were apart for their honeymoons. And not only that—to now also have the burden, and pain, of Bella's only child. Suddenly Auntie Dorothy looks very small to me, as if she has shrunk in just the two days since Auntie Bella's death. *It's not possible*, I think to myself. I look again. Then I see it's the chair she's sitting on, the low chair of the mourner—a little kindergarten chair that someone hauled up from Auntie Bella's basement (maybe even the same chair I sat on as Pearl's student)—and this has made my aunt into a miniature Auntie Dorothy, almost a midget. For the first time I see that she is not, as I have been telling myself, getting old; she *is* old. Someone smaller, and weaker, than I, someone who soon I will have to take care of.

Everyone is waiting for my answer, but still I haven't spoken. I resist at so many levels that I can barely name them all, and struggling through them is like drilling through all the different soils of the earth, layer after layer, down to the core, to the centre which is fire. And the fire says: "I love my aunt, I love this cousin, I am of this family, and I must do what I am asked."

I put down my teacup. I rise and slowly climb the stairs.

At the top, I knock on Pearl's door. I knock three times and wait, but there's no answer. Silence from inside the room, no music, no sound of any kind. Maybe she's sleeping. Maybe I shouldn't disturb—but to hell with this, she's my cousin, and suddenly I am angry at being shut-out by her, and I pound on the door, over and over, until finally it opens. There stands Pearl, calm

~
141

as you please, just mildly surprised to see me, as though I'd just dropped in, as if I always drop in from time to time. As if her mother's not dead, as though she hasn't got a living room full of guests downstairs, who have been eating and drinking and talking at forty decibels at least for most of the last two days.

"Oh, Eve," she says. "It's you. Come on in."

She opens the door wide and I enter.

Part Two

Her room is exactly as I remembered it. Along the left wall, one of the long sides of the rectangular room, is her single little girl's bed, and covering it is a woven, cream-coloured bedspread with a big, pink flower in the middle. Straight ahead is her white desk under the window; and down the right-hand side, all along the wall and even on the closet door halfway down, are posters, posters of Biafra, of Biafra's starving children. I remember when we all first heard about Biafra, when we first believed it, and understood that these were real people, not just pictures in *Life* magazine. That very week I started sending Canadian Friends of Biafra ten per cent of my weekly allowance. But Pearl sent *all* of hers. That was also the first time she decided to try going for a while without food. I recognize one of the posters from way back then, the one of the little girl who, like a shadow of Pearl, always looked down at us on the bed from her place on the closet door. She is about seven, with hungry haunting eyes and a swollen belly. She is wearing rags and stands barefoot on parched earth. Next to her on the wall is a poster of three children standing together. The oldest, a tall boy, has his arm around a girl, and on her other side, a small boy leans against her. Their bellies too are swollen, and their limbs look as brittle as flamingoes' legs. Behind them, in the doorway of a hovel, sits an emaciated old man with protruding ribs: their grandfather maybe, starving.

I skip over the rest of the posters and my eyes, drawn to the light, flit to something fastened to the wall between the window and the top of the desk. It is a yellowed piece of paper with something written on it in pencil and taped with tape so old it's brown. I don't need to step any closer to know what it is: It's Pearl's poem from grade seven, entitled "Death Shall Have No Dominion," for which she won a prize.

The room seems totally unchanged since I was last here. And so does Pearl from when I saw her most recently. I've seen her since high school of course, every couple of years when, home for a visit, I would drop in to Auntie Bella's before or after Auntie Dorothy's. Pearl would usually come down to the living room for a moment, out of curiosity it always seemed to me, the way people like from time to time to look at an animal in the zoo. She'd say hi, sometimes we'd kiss, we'd exchange pleasantries for a little while, and then she'd excuse herself and go back up to her room. So I am not surprised by her appearance. She is very skinny, she can't weigh more than ninety pounds, and her hair is shaved in a crewcut so short that through it you can see her scalp, like the earth breathing beneath cropped corn. She wears loose clothing—pants and a shirt—of coarse, colourless cotton, and like the girl in the poster, her feet are bare. She looks like a boy monk. (But consecrated to what?) Or a convict. (But what is her crime?) Or a survivor. (What has she survived? What brutalities have been visited upon her, that she looks like this?)

And yet her face, as she gazes calmly at me, is as direct, and clear, and honest as ever. And suddenly I am so glad to see her, I feel such a rush of cousinly affection for her, that I find myself smiling.

"Hi, Pearl," I say, and kiss her on the cheek. She kisses me back, and briefly we embrace like two old Greek widows, meeting again for the first time in many years, on the island that was their girlhood home. "I'm sorry about your mother," I say.

"Thanks."

She stands very still for a moment.

Then she says, "Come sit down," and she goes over to the bed and sits on it with her back to the window, cross-legged like a swami. "Come on," she says, and waves to me to join her.

I obey. I sit cross-legged as well, facing her like a mirror image. But then Pearl looks down and starts picking at the slubs on the old bedspread. I stare at her short-cropped head, and I realize suddenly that I do not know her, I do not know this lost, proud person, she is a stranger to me, and I have no idea what to say to her. I suppose I should be asking her in an avuncular, patronizing way (or an av*aunt*ular, matronizing way) what she wants to do with the rest of her life. But what seemed possible just moments ago downstairs, now feels impossibly insensitive, presumptuous, and crass.

Pearl looks up at me with the faintest of smiles. "So," she says. "They sent you to talk to me."

I feel myself blush, and immediately I am furious with myself, and then with her. "Well," I say stiffly, "they're worried about you."

"What are they saying?" she asks, looking right at me.

I look away—*what does she think I am, her spy?*—and study the white knobs on the drawers of her desk. I don't say a word.

"The biddies," she adds. "What do the biddies say?"

In spite of myself, I smile. Pearl always called them "the biddies," that older generation of women, all the aunties and sisters-in-law and cousins' wives and girlhood friends. Especially when they had their "hen parties," sitting around Auntie Bella's living room in the afternoons, drinking tea and nibbling on *mandelbroit*, talking and laughing, gossiping and telling stories until it was time to make supper for the men. Pearl always made me laugh afterwards up in her room with her imitations of Clara, Auntie Bryna's daughter, who tried to look prim and proper by pursing her lips and wrinkling her nose, but which only made her look as if she'd just smelled something bad.

"The biddies," I echo.

"I wish they'd mind their own business," says Pearl with sudden vehemence. "I'm not leaving this house, I don't care what plot they've got hatched. This house is mine, my mother left it to me."

I look at her in surprise.

"Uncle Herb wants me out of here, doesn't he?" she asks belligerently. I don't say anything. "That way he can turn this into an office and not have to go downtown any more. He can eat at home and save money on office space and lunches. I know how he thinks. I know how they all think."

The idea is quite plausible—I am surprised at its obviousness. But loyally I say, "Oh, I don't think so. Everyone just wants what's best for you."

She pauses, considering this for a moment, and then she looks at me. Her eyes soften a little.

"You're so naive, you know," she says. "Anyone else, I'd say they're lying to me. But I don't think you are. You just always see the good in people. You don't see them for how they really are."

"Yes, I do."

"No, you don't. You give them far too much credit. You think they're like you, you think everyone's like you, but they're not. You're kind, you always were, even when you were a little girl. But most people aren't, they don't care about anybody else, they only think about themselves. You're like me. You're sensitive. You *feel* things."

I am flattered to be included like this, along with Pearl, as one of the fine and feeling few in an obtuse and indifferent world, and delighted to discover that after all this time I still (or once again) have her approval, and respect. It is a little embarrassing how deeply this pleases and gratifies me, but it does. I can feel a warm stirring in my belly, like soft moss absorbing sun. And yet, a small thorn in the moss—her calling me naive. Who is she to judge me, anyway? What does she know about anything? I live in the world, and she is a hermit. A recluse. A reject. Like hell we're alike.

"I don't know," I say. "Maybe."

There is silence for a while, while Pearl picks away some more at the bedspread. Then she looks up at me mischievously.

"Do you remember Patsy Bomberg?" she asks.

Of course I do: Patsy Bomberg with her big fat bum and pointy Cossack boots and beehive-shaped hat; Patsy Bomberg who in grade seven made a club for all the girls on the street except us, a club for the girls like her, with all the latest clothes. Pearl and I smile at each other, our smiles stretch into grins, and we start to laugh. In a flash we are doubled over laughing, laughing laughing and laughing, totally helpless and out of control, and it feels so wonderful to laugh like this, even though I can't tell you exactly what it is that we're laughing about. It's better than crying, anyway. And such a relief after all that sadness and mourning, the plop plop plop of earth being thrown onto Auntie Bella's coffin six feet down in the ground. I feel something on my face. Still laughing, I reach up and touch it—to my surprise, it's tears; and laughing some more, I wipe them away from my eyes and cheeks.

Our laughter winds down, we struggle to catch our breath. We breathe deeply: one, two, three...Then Pearl asks, panting, "Do you remember that letter we wrote?" and we explode all over again, screeching with laughter like two young girls. One day, when our parents were out at a bar-mitzvah, Pearl and I wrote Patsy Bomberg a hate note. (Actually, to be exact about it, Pearl dictated it, and I wrote it down.) We told her that we hated her and we hated her club, and we were going to kill her the first chance we could get. (We didn't sign it, of course.) When we were finished, we snuck up to her house at the end of our street, giggling and blushing and egging each other on, amateur criminals that we were. We reached her front door and were about to stick the note through the mail slot, when we heard people moving around inside. "Quick!" Pearl stage-whispered. "Someone's coming!" Squealing with excitement, and pulling on each other's arms, we ran down the stairs, while Patsy's father opened the front door, stood there frowning, and watched us run away. Of course we took the note back home with us (what else could we do with it?), and we brought it upstairs and hid it in Pearl's room. Where is it now, I wonder? What ever happened to it? It's probably still around here someplace—odd to think of that little piece of hatred, buried nearly thirty years ago, somewhere so close to me now.

"Patsy Bomberg…" I say, still laughing, but suddenly I am very tired and dizzy. I haven't eaten anything all day, just tea and chocolate mints, and everything is starting to look strange and blurry: Pearl across from me, rocking and laughing to herself, looks like a laughing skull, a skull that's gone mad and will go on laughing forever. But then the skull transforms, and I see Pearl as she used to be back then: with a headful of curly brown hair, rosy cheeks, and eyes as boyishly daring as Peter Pan's. The two images, the skull and the girl, alternate, slowly at first and then more and more quickly, until finally they merge, superimposed on each other like a photo that's been double-exposed.

I am not laughing any more. The vision disappears, and I see my cousin sitting cross-legged in front of me, watching me close-ly. Studying me, even. When I meet her eyes, she says in a detached, clinical voice, as if giving me a diagnosis:

"You have the most wonderful laugh. My mother always said you had the sweetest laugh in the whole wide world. She always said, 'Why can't you be more like Eve, why can't you see the positive side of things?'"

I lower my eyes, her bitterness—as sharp and swift as a spear—slicing through my belly, through soft, unresisting flesh still warm from cousin-laughter; and it lands, ringing pain, in a deep inner bone. But I do not protest or argue with her. It is true what she says. I was Auntie Bella's god-daughter, and a little bit god-like to her—the perfect, prodigal, pretend-daughter. The one who married and had a family. Who had a career, and even appeared one time in the *Canadian Jewish News*.

"I loved her," I say, as if to apologize. "No, not loved—love. I haven't stopped loving her, just because—"

I stop. Still the dutiful god-daughter, I take seriously my role: Auntie Bella would want me to comfort, take care of, Pearl now. This is not the place, or time, to indulge my own grief. It is *her* mother, after all. Although I can't help thinking she didn't treat her much like one, she put her through every imaginable kind of hell. Those attempted suicides, the threats, the hurled accusations. My aunt's medications being flushed down the toilet in one of Pearl's fits of rage. The insults, the recriminations...blaming my aunt for everything: "It's because of *you* I've never had a boyfriend. Because of *you* I never got a job..." I heard them all second-hand, my aunt weeping and twisting a handkerchief in her fingers, twisting and turning and tormenting that handkerchief, until I put my hand over hers.

"Enough," I told Auntie Bella. "Enough. You'll drive yourself crazy, and it won't even do Pearl any good. We all make mistakes. Let it go—"

"But what if I'd tried harder? Given her ballet lessons? Taken her on trips? If only I'd fixed her up with someone, forced her to socialize more. But how can you force a child? She'd stand in the corner and cry: 'I don't want to go, don't make me go.' You'd have to have a heart of steel—but maybe I should've. Maybe that's what she needed—"

"No," I said firmly, and looked searchingly into my aunt's eyes, like trying to reach one of my patients, a lost person, a lost soul. Something in her eyes flickered back. "No," I said. "You did your best. You did okay. It's just the way she is. She's always been this way—"

"Yes," said my aunt with a sigh. "Yes, she has, even as a baby. Nothing made her happy."

She looked down for a moment. Then she looked back up at me with a valiant smile.

"So, tell me," she said, giving my hand a squeeze, "tell me about your Adam. What's he doing now? What's he learning in school? Oy, what a wonderful boy!"

And picturing Auntie Bella's ravaged face, with the big, dark circles under her eyes, and the shoeboxes full of pills for lowering her blood pressure and raising her spirits (as impossible as trying to lower and raise a flag at the same time), and all because of Pearl, I can't help being angry, furious even, at this skinny passive-aggressive adolescent before me, so absorbed in herself and her own pain. The short hairs sticking up uniformly all over her head, like a small bed of nails, may be the hair of the oppressed (of convicts, conscripts, and cancer patients); but it is also the hair of oppressors: of neo-Nazi hate groups, of G.I. Joes raping Asian girls, and of neighbourhood bullies at home. "The tyranny of the weak" is what this is: I've been here all of ten minutes, and already I feel bruised.

"She loved you, too," says Pearl, and for a moment I don't understand what she's talking about.

Then I do, and I shrug.

From downstairs we hear a wave of laughter—subdued, but laughter just the same. Someone must have told a joke, one of those morbid *shiva* house jokes, like the one my cousin Ron told this morning: "Why are lawyers buried thirty feet underground?" "Why?" everyone asked, except my cousin Michael who is a lawyer. "Because deep-down they're nice guys."

"Well," says Pearl, "someone's having a good time."

I shrug again. It's getting to be time for me to go back down. I can't take much more of this, I've had enough. We have nothing to say to each other now.

"What's it like down there, anyway?" Pearl asks.

"I don't know. A zoo. A lot of people coming by—everybody and their grandmother."

"Like who?"

I am surprised at her curiosity. In a monotone I run off a list of names.

"Anyone else?" she asks.

"Lots," I tell her, "but I don't remember their names. People I don't know...friends from your mother's sculpture class." Then I remember the man with the fedora who dropped by this morning. He put a hand on my arm, and said to me earnestly, "When you see Pearl—" "Oh!" I say. "There was someone who said to send you regards. Now what was his name? He said you knew his son..."

Pearl leans forward. "Ricky? Was his name Ricky?"

I try to remember. "No," I say slowly, "it wasn't Ricky. It was some Jewish name."

"Itchy? His father's name's Itchy."

I brighten up. "Yeah, that's it! Itchy. He said to send you his regards—"

"Oh!" cries Pearl. "Is he still here?"

"No. He left just after I came—around 12:30, 1..."

She is frantically twisting her hands. Then she brings her left hand to her mouth, and presses a knuckle against her teeth. Oddly familiar—I remember this gesture. From when she was afraid.

"What's wrong?" I ask.

"Nothing," she says. "Nothing." But her face is working in anguish, and she begins to gnaw on her knuckle. I watch her for a while biting herself.

"You're hurting it," I say.

She stops. She takes her hand away from her mouth. "Oh," she says. Then her eyes seem to clear, and they focus on me as if she has just noticed I am here. "Maybe you should go," she says.

I don't move.

"You know him," she says to me. "Ricky Kessler. He went with us to Penfield."

A vague picture forms, from thirty years ago at Penfield Elementary School: a slim, handsome boy, a little shy, with dark, wavy hair.

"He was older than us, wasn't he?" I ask. "In Howie's class...?"

"That's him," says Pearl. "Wait."

She gets up off the bed, goes over to the desk under the window, takes something from the top drawer, and hands it to me. It is an odd-shaped scrap of something—at first glance it looks like a piece of a puzzle.

"What's this?"

She turns it sideways, and I see I am holding a picture of a man cut out along the contours of his body, and whoever cut it out has also cut off his left arm just above the elbow. For a moment I study the small, serious face.

"He looks the same," I say. "It's amazing...what's he doing these days?"

"He's the National Director of CARE: Canadians for Animal Rights Education," Pearl says with pride.

"Really." I hesitate a bit, then ask as casually as I can, "How do you know him?"

Pearl shrugs. She takes the picture from my hand and puts it back in her desk. "It's a long story," she says.

I don't say anything. For a while there is silence.

Then I say, "I'm not in any hurry."

Pearl looks at me uncertainly.

"It's better than listening to the biddies," I add.

She laughs. "Well, *that's* true," she says. But then she looks doubtful again. "Are you sure? You don't have to be somewhere? Usually you're so busy—"

"I'm sure," I say.

"Well." She comes over to the bed, and sits back down, facing me. "You know," she begins, "how every February my mother and Auntie Dorothy go to Florida together for a week?" I nod.

She stops for a moment, and looks down. "*Went*. I mean went..." She stares at the bedspread for a while. Then she continues.

"Well, last February they went as usual. It's almost a year ago exactly—it was just a few days after my dog, Sydney, died—you knew about that?" I nod. "Well, that was on a Wednesday and they left on Friday. It was really really icy that day..."

Part Three

So Auntie Bella asked Pearl if she would help her get her suitcase down the stairs. She didn't really need to ask. Ice or no ice, once a year for the previous twenty-two years, ever since Uncle Harry died, Pearl had walked Auntie Bella next door to Auntie Dorothy's, carrying her bag, and from there Uncle Herb drove the two sisters to the airport. Auntie Bella's aqua suitcase was the old kind, heavy and hard-framed, without wheels—so Pearl hobbled with it two or three steps, put it down, rested, and lifted it again, over and over all the way there. Just after they got to the end of Auntie Bella's walkway, and turned right onto the city sidewalk, Pearl said what she said every single year, as if it were a totally new idea that had never occurred to her before, "Why Uncle Herb can't take his car out of the garage, and park it in front of our house, and help you with your suitcase once a year, I'll never understand."

And this year, like every year, Auntie Bella replied, "Now Pearl, you know what Dorothy has to go through just to get him to give us a lift."

It was an exceptionally cold day, and Pearl was wearing only a light windbreaker, not even zipped up. Auntie Bella watched her as Pearl stopped, put down the suitcase, rested a moment, and then bent down and picked it up again.

"You'll catch your death of cold," said Auntie Bella. Pearl didn't answer. They hobbled along, Auntie Bella being careful on the ice, Pearl busy with the suitcase.

Through the window Auntie Dorothy saw them coming up the path, and before they even reached the bottom of the stairs, she was at the door, opening it for them.

"Hello!" called Auntie Bella, and Auntie Dorothy waved back.

"I'll only stop in for a minute," Pearl said under her breath, exactly as she did every year. "And I won't stay if Uncle Herb is mean to me."

They climbed the six stairs carefully, holding onto the bannister, while Auntie Dorothy laughed and chattered to them from the doorway. At the top she kissed them, and they stepped into the warm vestibule. But even before Auntie Dorothy shut the door behind them, Pearl sensed her mistake. There were two strange men, one older and one younger, in the shadowy hallway ahead of them, and there was no chance of escape. The older man had already come over and was kissing Auntie Bella on the cheek.

"Bella Hirschman! I haven't seen you in—Good Lord!—it must be thirty-five years! How wonderful to see you. I hear you and Dorothy are on your way to Florida—"

"Itchy Kessler! I don't believe it," gushed Auntie Bella. "Oh Pearl, you don't remember...When you were just a baby, Itchy and Ethel and Ricky used to come up with the Malins to the country...How are you?" she asked Itchy. "I hear from Dorothy you've been doing some legal work for Herb."

"Yes—we just dropped by, in fact, to pick up some papers."

Auntie Bella suddenly noticed the young man standing in the shadows behind Itchy. "Oh!" she cried. "This must be Ricky!"

Ricky stepped forward into the light, and Pearl immediately recognized him. He was slim, smooth, and sophisticated now, but he had the same shy smile he'd had in grade five, standing alone in the schoolyard at recess, his hands in his pockets. He was different then from the other boys in his class. A nice boy, not rough. A boy whose mother was dying. Everyone knew and whispered behind his back. None of the other boys ever threw the ball to him, to include him in a game of pitch-and-catch. As though death itself were catchy.

Ricky shook Auntie Bella's hand. "Nice to see you again, Mrs. Hirschman," he said.

"Oh Ricky," cooed Auntie Bella, and laughing, she shook her head. "Just look at you."

Then Ricky noticed Pearl. "I know you," he said. "I'm sure of it. Don't we know each other from somewhere?"

He was handsome. And he looked, oddly enough, a little like her father, or anyway like his picture next to Pearl's bed, from just before he died. In the picture he was standing next to his horse, his hand on its damp, chestnut flank; he was wearing a riding cap and breeches, and holding a whip, and smiling straight into the camera. Just like Ricky was smiling at her now.

Pearl nodded.

"From Penfield?" he asked, and smiling, she nodded again.

"So Ricky," said Auntie Bella, "are you helping your father in the firm?"

Itchy laughed. "Oh no! He's way too smart for that! He works for the Animal Protection Society. He's the National Director for all of Canada."

Auntie Bella and Auntie Dorothy looked suitably impressed.

"Canadians for Animal Rights Education," Ricky corrected his father.

"Whatever," said Itchy, and turned back to the ladies. "He's just here for the week from Ottawa, for the international conference on animal rights. Yesterday he gave the keynote address."

"I can't find those deeds, Dorothy," said Uncle Herb, coming up the stairs from the basement.

"Now," said Itchy, "if he'd only make an old man happy—settle down, have a family—"

"Dad!"

"Oy, you see what I'm up against?" groaned Itchy to the two older ladies, who smiled sympathetically. "Kids these days..."

"Dorothy," said Uncle Herb, "did you ask Bella if maybe she's got them?"

"Not yet, dear...Bella, you remember the deeds of sale to your house and ours, we kept them together?" Auntie Bella nodded. "Well, Herbie would like Itchy to take a look at them while we're away—there's some problem with the property line—and we can't find them. Do you think maybe you have them at home?"

"Gee, I don't know," said Auntie Bella. "You mean right now to go look for them? I don't want us to be late for the plane."

"I can get them," volunteered Pearl, "if you tell me where they are."

Auntie Bella looked at her doubtfully. "Well," she said, "I'm not even sure I have them. But if I do, they would probably be where I keep all my important papers. You know, in the kitchen—"

"Oh, yeah," said Pearl. "Behind the cookie jar."

"Behind the cookie jar!" muttered Uncle Herb.

"Sssh," said Auntie Dorothy.

"That's right," Auntie Bella said to Pearl. "Where I keep all the bills—"

"They look like this," said Uncle Herb, holding up a long, legal page full of very small print. "Exactly like this, but this is just a copy. We need the originals."

"It should say Malin and Kessler at the top," Itchy chimed in.

"Well," said Pearl, "if they're there, they shouldn't be hard to find."

"Why don't I go with you?" Ricky said to Pearl. "I know what they look like. And that way you don't have to go and come back. I can just bring them home with me tonight," he said to his father, "after the conference..."

"Sounds great," said Itchy.

"Now Pearl," said Auntie Bella, "if we have them, they'll be right where I put the electricity bill this morning."

"I know, I know," said Pearl.

"And do up your jacket."

"Ma!"

Ricky laughed and looked at Pearl. Confused, she lowered her eyes.

"Do you have your car here?" Ricky asked her. "We could take mine, if you want—I've rented—"

He broke off. Everyone was laughing, except him. He stood there looking perplexed, vulnerable even, until Auntie Dorothy explained:

"They live next door! Actually, our two houses are attached—we share a living room wall—that's why we did the deeds together."

Ricky smiled appreciatively, and nodded.

"Some people think it's a little crazy," said Auntie Bella, "living in each other's pockets like this. But we're a close family, it suits us fine."

"Nothing wrong with being close," said Ricky, smiling.

Then he turned to Pearl. "I guess we'd better get started on our long trek."

"Pearl, do up your coat," said Auntie Bella.

"Goodbye, Ma," said Pearl. "Have a good trip." She kissed her on the cheek.

"See you later," Ricky said to his dad. "Nice to meet you all..."

"You, too..."

⋅⊱⊱═◉═⊰⊰⋅

The two young people walked out, the four old people watching them.

"Are you sure you're not cold?" asked Ricky, as they walked down Auntie Dorothy's snow-lined path.

"No, really," said Pearl and looked away when he tried to catch her eye. At the end of Auntie Dorothy's walkway, they turned left onto the city sidewalk.

"You know," said Pearl impulsively, "I think the work you do, protecting animals, is really really important."

"Thank you," said Ricky, looking surprised. "So do I, actually."

"Your mother, did she love animals, too?" asked Pearl.

"My mother?"

"Yeah, your mother."

"I don't know," said Ricky, looking confused. "I don't remember."

"I remember when she died," said Pearl.

"You do?" Ricky turned sharply to look at her, and at the same time they made another left onto Auntie Bella's walkway.

"Yes," said Pearl. "After that you were always alone at recess, and you wore the same red sweater, this sleeveless pullover, every single day."

"Did I?" He made a laughing sound but his eyes didn't laugh. "A red pullover..." he said wonderingly, and frowned.

They climbed the six stairs to the house, and Ricky paused at the top, waiting for Pearl to unlock the door. But she just pushed it open and walked inside. Ricky followed close behind her.

"I'll get you those deeds, if I can find them," said Pearl, and slipping off her wet shoes, walked straight ahead into the kitchen. She came back a few moments later. Ricky was standing in the vestibule, in his long grey coat and dripping boots, watching her walk towards him.

"Here they are," said Pearl, and handed him a brown envelope. "They were right where she said they'd be."

"Thanks," he said, sliding it into the inside pocket of his coat. "I'll give it to my dad."

Pearl nodded.

But then, instead of leaving, Ricky stood there and looked at her, his head lowered and looking up at her, and cocked slightly to one side like a squirrel's. He smiled at her, and in spite of herself, Pearl felt herself smile back.

"Maybe I could come in for a minute?" Ricky suggested. "I have a little time till I have to be back at the conference, I'm not in a rush. Unless, of course, you are in the middle of something..."

Pearl hesitated. Even the slightest bit of pressure, the slightest lack of respect...But there was neither of these. "Well," she said. "I guess for a minute..."

"Great," said Ricky. He kicked off his boots and lightly tossed them onto the rubber mat in the corner.

"Would you like some tea?" asked Pearl, doing what her mother always did with guests.

"Sure," and he followed her into the kitchen in his stockinged feet. With his coat still on but open, he stood watching her as she filled the kettle with water from the tap, placed it on the stove, turned on the gas flame, and took down from the white-painted cupboards a tin of Earl Grey tea, a teapot with pink flowers on the side, and two cups and saucers with the same design. Into the teapot she carefully spooned some tea.

"This is delightful," said Ricky, slipping off his coat and throwing it over the back of a kitchen chair. This house, he told Pearl, was exactly the same layout as the one he'd grown up in eight blocks away. It felt wonderful, he said, to be back in the old neighbourhood, and to see an old friend again after all these years. And he couldn't remember when he'd felt so immediately at home, as if he had known her all his life.

"That's cause you have," said Pearl.

Ricky looked surprised, then he laughed. "You're right," he said, and Pearl smiled. She felt completely natural, too, standing around the kitchen with him, waiting for the water to boil. As if he was just another old friend of the family, the son of one more of her mother's childhood friends—or even one of the slew of male cousins that she grew up with. But along with this, the thought kept coming up—like the after-taste she used to get in her mouth all morning long, after eating eggs for breakfast—that of course this wasn't natural at all. It was totally unnatural to feel this way, to feel so at home with a stranger. She told this voice to shut up, though, this high-pitched girlish voice of fear and caution, of Little Red Riding Hood and big bad wolves. "Shut up," she told it. It was always holding her back, ruining her fun, keeping her from doing things she wanted to do. Not to it, but to Ricky she listened, while he told her all about his work: the things he liked about it and the things he didn't. He hated the traveling, for instance, flying from one end of Canada to the other, four times a year, to fundraise for CARE. He hated hotels, and restaurant meals, and always having to be "on." And as he spoke she felt a strange but soothing sensation, a kind of rocking, like being on a boat, though she had never been on a boat, but it felt like that, she was sure it was like that, the rocking of a boat. Back and forth, back and forth...

"Oh it's not all bad," he was saying to her with warmth. "Some of the places I go to are wonderful. Vancouver, for instance, is so beautiful. You would love Vancouver."

Pearl was next to the stove, leaning with the small of her back against the kitchen counter, and Ricky was standing in the middle of the kitchen on the blue and yellow-tiled floor, and talking with his hands. "The scenery, the mountains, the people," he said, "they're just incredible. You wouldn't believe it, it's another world. I could take you to an artists' colony there that I was at. You should see these aboriginal artists, they live completely in harmony with nature. Not like here, where everything's so materialistic and artificial."

These were two of Pearl's key words. Everyone has key words—words that encapsulate their most essential hates and loves. *Materialistic. Artificial.* Things that Pearl hated. Using these words, Ricky was speaking her real, inner language; he had the key to her code.

"It sounds amazing," said Pearl, her eyes shining.

"Oh it is."

The kettle whistled. Slowly Pearl turned around, lifted it from the stove, and poured its steaming, gurgling water into the teapot.

"Should we have it in here," she asked, "or in the living room?"

"Oh, anywhere. I don't care."

"Well, in there then," she said. She lifted the two cups and saucers and gently held them out to him, the way her mother always handed things to her, like offering a gift. Ricky slipped his coat over his arm and accepted the cups and saucers from Pearl. She herself carried in the tray with the matching teapot, sugar bowl and creamer and a small plate of her mother's *mun* cookies.

"So you live here with your parents?" he asked, walking ahead of her towards the sofa.

Pearl kept her eyes focussed on his back, on one single point in the middle of his white shirt, a trick she learned once, to help her keep her balance. Then Ricky stopped and bent over to put down the cups, and watching him, she nearly toppled—but then she bent over too, and together they set everything down on the polished mahogany coffee table in front of the old green couch. Pearl sneaked a look at his face as he sat down on the sofa not too far from her on her right. No, he didn't look sarcastic, it didn't seem he was being snarky with his question.

"It's just me and my mum," she answered. "She needs me here since my father died."

He turned to her, his eyes flashing with quick empathy. "I know what you mean," he said. "My father really shouldn't be alone, either. I try to visit as often as I can, but I don't get here as much as I'd like."

"He seems to be doing okay," said Pearl.

"Well...He's happy now that I'm here for the week. But he's getting old. He's starting to forget things...And everything falls on my sister just 'cause she lives down the block from him."

"Oh, I'm sure he understands how busy you are," Pearl said ardently. "You have such an important job. Anyway, you're lucky you have a sister to share it with. With us there's only me and my mum. It's harder being all alone."

Ricky looked at Pearl now with a new intensity, as if seeing her for the first time. He brought his face closer to hers, and looked into her eyes.

"It's not good to be alone," he said. "People weren't meant to be alone."

His eyes were brown and deep and compassionate, and she knew, looking into them, that he understood, really understood, what it was like for her. Then he raised his hand to her cheek, and held it there, looking at her like someone who loved her, who'd always loved her, who understood everything without the need for words.

Frightened, she pulled away.

"You're shy," he said softly.

She shrugged, staring down at the carpet.

"So am I," said Ricky.

"You?!" Amazement overpowered her fear, and she looked up at him, disbelieving. "But you—you're so sociable...You're good with people, you're a 'National Director.' You talk to people all the time."

"Oh, maybe it seems like that. I have learned, of course, how to talk to people, how to get along, I've had to for my work. But a lot of that is just a big bag of tricks. Inside, I'm actually much more like you."

"Oh, yes?" asked Pearl. "And how do you know what I'm like inside?"

"Oh I don't...I mean, I hardly know you. But I can...I can feel how sensitive you are, how shy. How deeply you feel things. I'm like that, too, though I rarely let it show."

"Really?"

"Really."

He smiled at her. Shyly, gratefully, she smiled back. And as he looked at her, a yearning, a kind of pain, came over his face.

"You're so different from all the other women I know," he said. "So unpretentious, and natural, and real. I feel so at home with you, like I can just be myself—"

Suddenly his face was buried in her breasts, and his arms were tight around her, needing her, clinging to her. She didn't push him away, but sat there, confused and dazed, feeling his face pressing against her breast. Vaguely she reached out for his hair, to stroke him, to comfort him, the way she used to stroke her dog Sydney on the top of his head. But once she felt Ricky's wavy black hair in her fingers, she pulled him tighter to her, and tighter yet, and she felt him close against her...

Then with both hands she pushed him away. His face, flushed and strange-looking like a Loch Ness monster rising from the deep, rose slowly from between her breasts; and as the rest of him straightened back up, his eyes looked for hers, found them, and locked into them, full of desire. Pearl stared back at him in shock, with the same look as if she had just been struck across the face with the flat of his hand.

Ricky smiled at her tenderly. "Sshhh," he said, as she tried to speak. "Sshhh."

He reached up and touched her cheek. Then he said, "Soon I have to go," and she nodded—but she nodded without removing her eyes from his. She stared at him, transfixed.

"I have to go," he said again. "There's an evening session I have to go to."

Pearl didn't nod this time. She just continued to stare at him, dumbly, steadily, like a child.

A little impatient now, Ricky rose, his right hand holding his coat; with the other he raised Pearl to her feet and led her over to the vestibule. There he pulled on his boots and slipped into his coat. He smiled at her, and kissed her softly on the forehead.

And then he opened the door, shut it behind him, and was gone.

→·⊨══◉══⊨·←

After he left she went upstairs and sat cross-legged on her bed, her back to the window, staring straight in front of her. Her eyes were wide and frightened, like a deer startled on the road at night by the headlights of a car in its eyes. For a long time she stared absently in front of her, biting the knuckle on the index finger of her left hand. This was her position: this was how she sat when she was in her half-state, that state that was not awake and not asleep, but somewhere in-between, an in-between place where she spent almost all of her time. She was in this place now, listening to another language, something that most people never hear—just as they never hear the high pitch of a dog whistle, and so they don't believe it's really making a sound. Deeply Pearl was listening, deeply she was floating in that place that felt like underwater, deep down, just above the ocean floor. Underwater where the density was different, the intensity was different, from the everyday, normal world. There was darkness, and silence, and the breathing of the deep.

Down here she was at home, it was as familiar to her as the underwater world to a deep-sea diver, and like a diver, she longed for this place when too long away from it, when she remained too long at the surface of things, at the surface of the water, at that exact point that divides water from air, inside from out. Sometimes, when forced too long to be in "the real world," to be with people, in the normal and the everyday, Pearl became breathless. She literally gasped, like a fish out of water, begged to be excused, and fled to her room.

This was the place she had come to ever since she could remember, since she was three years old, and so lonely that she made friends with the air, the air slowly wafting from the squat, iron heater in the basement. She felt it warm against her face, and in the basement's dark dampness, she knew from this warmth that she was real, and alive, because something was touching her, she could feel it on her skin. Next she made friends with the basement clock, the old-fashioned wooden clock on the mantelpiece, with its loud, steady ticking that told her she was not alone. And she made friends with time itself: she learned to hear the silent passing of time, she could tell you the exact time, within a minute or two, any time of the day or night, without ever looking at a watch. (Her male cousins would test her, they'd interrupt her in the middle of a game of Parcheesi or Scrabble, and ask her what time it was, and she'd look up and blink and tell them the correct time with no effort at all, as though she was answering "What is your name?") After that she made friends with everything, because everything is alive, everything is connected, and you are not really separate from anything in the world. She learned this from a book that someone read to her once, about a Navajo girl for whom everything was alive, even rocks and trees, earth and sky: She talked to them all, and they helped her when she was in trouble, once they even saved her life. Everything became Pearl's friend, alive and breathing: everything had feelings, even bread being cut with a knife. Even the bricks on the wall being painted over with thick light-green paint. "I can't breathe, I can't breathe!" the bricks screamed, but no one else heard it but her, and the grown-ups laughed when she told them; she wailed and sobbed, but they kept on painting. She heard people screaming, too, people screaming with hunger, far away; and people in her own house, fighting: her father's shouts and the thud of things being thrown; the silent scream of her mother's pain.

Pearl floated. She floated safe in her ocean, among slowly

moving, primal currents. In the warm, dark ocean, the anemones gracefully, and hypnotically, waved. Everything was going to be all right.

⊷▬◉▬⊶

The next day, Ricky came over after work. He stood in the vestibule, unwrapping his scarf from around his neck. Then he took off his coat, handed it to Pearl, and smiled at her. She could barely look at him: she looked away and turned around with his coat toward the closet.

"What is it?" asked Ricky. "What's wrong? You won't even look at me."

Pearl shook her head, hanging up his coat. When she turned around again, Ricky was standing right in front of her, and looking for her eyes. He found them, and quickly she lowered them.

"You're shy with me?" Ricky asked softly.

Pearl shrugged.

"Don't be," he said and smiled at her. She looked back up at him, and whatever she saw there reassured her.

"Take it easy," he said. "We'll just have a cup of tea, okay?, if that's what you want."

Pearl nodded.

"Fine," said Ricky. "No problem. Friends, right?"

Pearl nodded again. They smiled at each other. Then they grinned; and laughing with relief she led him into the kitchen, where she had already laid out the tea set, and the cookies, and the cups and saucers. Ricky chatted to her as she made the tea, the same as the day before, and when it was ready, they again carried it into the living room, and sat on the couch, waiting for it to steep. After a few minutes Pearl poured it, as formally as in a Japanese tea ceremony, and they took their first sips together in ritualistic silence. Then Pearl asked Ricky about his work, and listened closely, nodding, as he talked about the meeting he had just come from, and how he'd been stabbed in the back, betrayed, by a young man whom he had actually helped bring up through the ranks, and who now headed the Montreal branch and was always trying to turn the others against him. Suddenly Ricky stopped.

"Enough about that," he said. He turned to face Pearl, and smiled at her. "The jungle—all that's a million miles away. Here I am in a quiet glade. An oasis. One of the last unpolluted islands in the world."

Pearl smiled back and then looked down.

Ricky watched her affectionately. "You know what you're like?" he asked. "You remind me of one of those rare, shy birds we're trying to save in Temagami—the only surviving cousin of the dodo bird."

"Thanks," said Pearl.

"No, I mean it. Look at you, how beautiful you are. How unique. I've never met anyone quite like you before."

She looked up at him, frowning. He wasn't laughing at her. He looked completely sincere.

He leaned forward and touched her cheek. "I want to get to know you," he said emotionally. "I want to know everything about you—how you think, how you feel. I want you to tell me everything."

Pearl shrugged, looking down and blushing. "There's not much to tell," she said. "I don't have a job or anything like that. I take care of my mother. I lead a very simple life."

"Oh no," said Ricky, "I don't believe that for a moment. There is so much inside of you, so much depth and understanding. So much feeling. You are more alive than anyone else I know."

He took her hand, and while she watched him, he examined it closely, as if he'd never seen a hand before. Then he turned it upward, brought it to his mouth, and kissed her palm. Then each of her fingers one at a time. Then her wrist, and all around her wrist in a circle.

Frightened, she pulled her hand away. "Can't we just talk?" she asked.

"Sure," he said, letting go of her hand. "What about?"

About you, she thought. *Like how you came to be the way you are: so gentle, and beautiful, and strong. So open with your feelings. So fearless. Whereas I—I am afraid all the time. You must teach me how to be more like you.*

But aloud she only said, "Oh, I don't know. Anything. About you."

"I don't like declarations," Ricky declared, and he leaned back in his handsome green Ralph Lauren sweater, clasping his hands together behind his head and stretching out his legs straight in front of him. "I like the stories to come out by themselves."

Pearl pondered this for a moment. "Well, then," she said, "just tell me something small. Anything."

"Ask me a question."

"Oh, I don't know." She stared at the motif on his sweater: a man on his horse. "Are you happy?" she asked him.

Ricky laughed. "Now *there's* a small question! Happy?! I'm happy right *now*," he said. He leaned forward and took her hand in his. "You can't imagine..." he said, his voice thickening.

"I can," said Pearl. "Because I am, too."

"Really?"

"Really."

They grinned at each other. But then, all of a sudden, Pearl began to feel like she was disappearing again. Her smile faded, she sank underwater. And from there, hypnotized and passive, she watched Ricky, waiting for him to do something.

Ricky leaned forward and kissed her on the cheek. She smiled.

"Your cheek," he said. He kissed her on her forehead. "Your fore-head," he said. He kissed her on each of her eyes and on her nose ("Your eyes. Your nose")—and then softly, with his lips, and his tongue, he kissed her on the mouth.

He loves me, thought Pearl. *He doesn't want to hurt me.* But still she felt that stiffness in her body, that holding back, as he con-tinued to kiss her, on her neck, and her shoulder, and all the way down her arm. She was watching from outside herself, she was recording it as it went along, as if for a later purpose. He was doing this to her, that to her, or anyway to her body. This felt good, this didn't, and this didn't feel anything at all, but she didn't dare ask him to stop. He might get angry, he might hit her. Not that anyone had ever hit her, not that she could remember any-way, but it was not her that was thinking these things. It was her body, her body remembering, remembering something buried in her flesh, in the language of the body, years before—and re-awak-ened now by Ricky's particular touch.

Pearl watched from outside, from above, like God watching from a cloud in the heavens. A man was making love to her. It couldn't be happening, but it was. He was caressing her up and down her inner arm, he was playing with her hands. Now he was slowly tracing the neckline of her shirt, the place where cloth meets skin, as respectful of this line as if it were a border. But then he very softly ran his fingers over her left breast and watched her face change. Pearl shut her eyes, she let herself feel it. He contin-ued to stroke her, back and forth, back and forth, and she could feel, even through the cotton blouse, his fingers on her nipple. Suddenly she was panting, and her body began to move of its own accord, like something independent of her.

"No. No. I can't," she said, and pushed Ricky away.

A moment passed. "It's all right," he said, "it's okay." He

reached out and put his arms around her. "There's no rush," he said. "We have time, we have all the time in the world." And he held her tenderly, as if holding something precious, like a prehistoric vase.

She nestled against him, and he stroked her short-cropped hair.

"You think I'm stupid," she said.

"No."

"I'm sorry."

"Never mind. It's nothing. Ssshh..." and he kissed her on the forehead.

Eventually he said, "Soon, I'm going to have to go." Pearl said nothing and didn't move, as if she hadn't heard.

After a bit, Ricky began to extricate himself from her, gently but firmly loosening her arms from around him, and sitting her up, like a doll, a little away from him on the couch. In this position, Pearl noticed the coffee table and the tea things on it.

"We didn't finish our tea," she said.

Surprised, Ricky looked over at the cups of tea still three-quarters full. "You're right," he said. He smiled at Pearl. "Tell you what then—to make up for today, tomorrow we'll drink double."

"Yes," she said.

Then Ricky rose, and as Pearl started walking him to the door, everything seemed perfectly normal, absolutely normal and everyday, she was just walking someone to the door. But then, all of a sudden, it didn't seem normal at all. There was nothing normal about this. He was her body—how could he be leaving her, how could he be walking away from her? Why was he putting on his coat? Why was he preparing to walk out that door?

But then Ricky turned to her with a smile, took both her hands in his, and kissed her on the cheek.

Pearl smiled back, no longer afraid.

And then he was gone.

⤙═◉═⤚

All night she didn't sleep. Her body was awake, he'd awakened it from a long deep sleep, like Sleeping Beauty. His kisses were still fresh, she felt them, she relived them and now she didn't want to sleep any more; she wanted to feel, feel everything, all the sensations in her body.

In a thin flannel nightgown she lay on her bed. Over and over she felt again his lips soft and then hard against hers, and his fingers lightly stroking her breast. Pleasure. And at the same time, illogically, pain—a faint, insistent ache rising from inside her skin. At sunrise she dozed off and dreamed of her underwater world. The ocean was filled with wonderful fish in all different colours, magnificent luminous blues, and yellows, oranges, reds and golds. But all of them were bruised somehow: one had a slightly mashed-in head; another swimming by had a sick, eggplant-coloured stain along its broadside, disturbing the perfect pin-stripe pattern in yellow and blue. And the plants were wounded, too: there were broken leaves, and crushed coral, and the transparent anemone was truncated, like an arm missing a hand. Eerily it waved, like the ghostly greeting of an amputee.

Then out of the blue, words appeared in the water, floating by like strange fishes. Some of them made no sense at all; some did—and others yet transmuted, changing into other words before her very eyes: *Kiss*, swimming by in thick purple letters, became *kick. Kiss, kick*—only one sound apart—as close as cousins. And then *kiss* reversed, *kiss* became *sick,* and *sick* became *suck*...and *sock*, and *sack*, and *seek*—"sk" being one of those magic consonant-pairs that works with all the vowels, every one making a real word. Then these words formed sentences, and in her sleep, Pearl read, like a primer, a different story about Dick and Jane: *It*

~
171

is sick to suck. Sick to seek. Sick to seek, suck, or sock someone in the sack.

The fish swam indifferently in and out of the letters, as if these were just another strange but unthreatening form of life. Sometimes they bumped into the words, and when that happened they just bounced off them as though they were made of rubber, and floated around for a bit in wordless space. After a while, the words began breaking up into separate letters, and then these letters thinned out and receded, as though they'd migrated to another ocean to spawn. And soon there were only a few letters floating around, and then there were only two, and then there were none. The water became warmer then, and an unclouded, beautiful green. And as Pearl watched, the purplish bruise faded away on the blue and yellow pin-striped fish, and the head of the other one filled out, returning to its original, God-given shape, and the hand of the anemone grew back, miraculously whole once again, under her believing eyes. The magic water had healed them all.

⋅⇥⊜⇤⋅

Ricky came over the next day, and the next day, and the next three days after that; and each day he brought a little more of her to life: An arm. A shoulder. A breast. Her mouth. Her thighs. They always began the evening standing around the kitchen while Pearl made them tea; and Ricky, who'd just come in from the February cold outside, seemed to breathe in the warmth of the house with a pleasure almost proprietary, as if he were a husband come home to his wife and they were about to have their supper together. It felt almost as natural as that, even after such a short time. When everything was ready, he helped her carry the tea things into the living room, and they sat on the couch; ceremoniously she poured out the dark, hot tea, and they sipped in silence until they were done. Then they put down their teacups, and Ricky turned toward Pearl and smiled at her. Tremblingly she smiled back, and he kissed her on the mouth, lightly, gently. Then more insistently—and she leaned back and let him stroke her. It was no longer *I want him, but I am afraid*; now it was *I am afraid, but I want him*. She wanted him to touch her and kiss her everywhere. And he did—almost. There were certain limits they both accepted, as if instead of 41, she was really 14, and (without ever talking about it) they'd agreed on how far a good girl should go. At the end of each evening, their clothes in disarray, they were flushed and intimate on the old green couch.

Afterwards, they sat up and talked. Or rather, Pearl talked to Ricky. She wanted to tell him everything, she wanted him to know everything about her. His eyes were warm, like sunlit alfalfa honey, and they beckoned, they drew her in to them, like honey to a sweetness-starved fly. Ricky listened to Pearl with his full attention on her, nodding from time to time, and occasionally giving an appreciative laugh. He listened intently, with his face close to hers, as though afraid of missing a single word, and as she spoke he looked at her as if she were the most amazing person he had ever met. Pearl had never before been listened to like this. She had never felt so important, and interesting, and loved. Everything she said he seemed to understand—he didn't think she was strange or crazy at all. And not only did he consider her okay, and the equal of the other girls he knew (normal girls, the Patsy Bombergs of the world who hadn't invited her into their club); he placed her way above them. He thought she was special; and all the differentness in her, as far as he was concerned, was only a matter for praise. He didn't think she was too serious, too intense, or too smart, as the boys had in high school. Her brilliance and intensity excited him. As did her body. She was a wonderful lover, sensuous, responsive, and passionate, and he told her so. Under all this admiration and tenderness, Pearl became a different person than she'd ever been before. Ricky opened a door inside her that had been locked; he freed her as if she were a genie trapped in a bottle, waiting all these years to get out.

For this she loved him. For creating her, for holding up to her this magic mirror of herself, a mirror that resided only in his eyes. It was only because of him that this wonderful new her existed. And this itself was just a minute reflection of his own wonderfulness. It was only from standing in the glow of his beauty and charisma that some little bit of it rubbed off on her—the bits she saw reflected in his eyes. Without him she'd be nothing, just as the sea turns black when the moon above it is gone. Without him she wouldn't *be*.

⊷≖◉⊜≖⊶

On the last day of his visit, after the sun had set, Ricky walked up the path to Pearl's house. His bags were waiting in the back seat of the little red rental car, in his pocket was a ticket for the 8:00 Rapidair to Ottawa, and Pearl was underwater, at the bottom of the ocean. She didn't know how this had happened exactly; just that about a half-hour before, she'd decided not to swim back up. She thought she would let him see her, who she really was, she would give him this parting gift. But now as he was about to arrive, she panicked. She didn't know how to be with people when she was like this. She didn't know how to talk, much less banter. She was six years old again, at a party of her parents': awkward and speechless when the fancy-dressed guests, smelling of liquor and perfume, bent down to her height, and clinking the ice in their glasses of Scotch, asked her how she was doing in school.

When the doorbell rang, Pearl was still sitting cross-legged on her bed, staring straight in front of her and biting on her knuckle. She leaped up guiltily, as though she'd been doing something wrong, and ran to let Ricky in.

His lips against her cheek were cold from outside. She took his coat. She hung it up. She led him into the kitchen. She did all the normal things; but everything was done in a trance (*Does he notice? Can he tell?* she wondered) and even though he was talking ("The closing session ran over...I couldn't get away...My plane leaves at 8..."), it was all somewhat unreal, far away, like the sounds you hear around you when you're swimming. Her cousin Howie had noticed once when she was like this. She was sixteen at the time, and he was eighteen and already into drugs. "I know what it is about you!" he'd said, after studying her for a while at a family gathering. "You're naturally stoned. You're stoned all the time, aren't you, even without dope!" She'd wondered then, and afterwards, if he was right, and if this was what it was like with dope; and if so, why people needed it so much, when they could just slide underwater anyway without it, anytime they wanted.

I'm not crazy, she thought, reaching up to the cupboard and taking down the tin of tea, *just "naturally stoned."* And this cheered and steadied her a bit, as she put the water on to boil, and spooned the tea leaves into the teapot, with Ricky's eyes all the while fixed on her back. With relief she felt her deep, heavy breathing lighten into shallower, more normal breaths. But even so, everything seemed to be moving slowly, very slowly and strangely, like the hot air wafting from the iron heater of her childhood, or the waving of anemones on the floor of the ocean, anemones waving goodbye. Pearl, too, began moving more and more slowly, like a clock gradually winding down until it stops...moving...altogether. Her hand rested on the tin of tea on the counter, and her head was slightly bowed.

Soundlessly Ricky came up behind her, and she felt his arms around her waist. He turned her around to face him, took her in his arms and held her. After a long time, Pearl spoke in a dreamy voice: "I've never touched you, you know. You've touched me, but I've never touched you."

Ricky didn't answer, but his head slightly drooped.

Pearl's face stayed buried in his sweater, turned away to the right, and for a while she didn't move. But then her left hand reached up and touched his hair. Tenderly, slowly, she ran her fingers through it, then over his ear, and down his cheek, feeling with the tips of her fingers the slight stubble, and the warm skin underneath it yielding to her touch. She was tracing him—tracing him to know him, to remember him, the way a blind person, relying on what is felt, feels you in order to know you. She touched his mouth, beginning to trace the beautiful softness of his lips, but they tried to close around her fingers, snapping at them like a Venus' fly-trap, trying to suck them in. Quickly she pulled away, but Ricky's hand seized hers and pressed it back against his lips.

"I want you so much," he said into her fingers. "I need you." Then he looked up into her eyes. "Our last day," he said.

Pearl nodded.

Silently he placed his hand between her legs.

"Please," he said.

Pearl stared in front of her for a moment, feeling the warm pressure of his hand. Then she looked down and moved his hand away. But now he was standing there, waiting, and she felt she owed him an explanation. She didn't want him to think she didn't love him, she didn't want him to feel rejected, he might get angry. But also she didn't want him to think that she was a freak, someone who was forty-one years old and had never done this before—who'd never even taken all her clothes off in front of a man. She cast about frantically for the right thing to say, and finally settled on Ricky's own word—a good word, a normal word, denoting gentleness and old-fashioned modesty in the style of Annette Funicello—and nothing of pathology or fear.

"I'm sorry, I can't," she said. "I'm still...shy."

It was a good choice. He responded to it emotionally. "I know," he said. "So am I." There was a pause and then he added, "No. More than that. I'm afraid."

Pearl looked up at him in amazement. She had never in her life heard a man (or a woman, for that matter) admit to being afraid, and she was deeply moved. She put a hand on his arm.

"But why?" she asked. "You've done this before."

There was a pause while Ricky, looking down, struggled for words. "This is different," he said at last. "This is...*meaningful*."

Then he looked at her, and his face was the face that she had remembered: the boy in the schoolyard, newly motherless, uncertain, dazed.

"For me, too," said Pearl.

Ricky nodded, and suddenly he looked exhausted. They stood for a moment without speaking. Then Ricky said, "Let's have some tea."

Pearl smiled, nodding. He couldn't have said anything more perfect, anything that would have shown more completely his understanding of her, his acceptance and respect. She was about to reach up and place her palm flat against his cheek, when just then the kettle started to screech, as if answering Ricky. Pearl turned around, switched off the stove, and busied herself happily at the counter—at first with just an inward smile, and then an outward one, a big, real smile breaking across her face. *"This is different,"* he'd said. *"This is meaningful..."* When everything was ready, she turned around and offered Ricky the cups and saucers; he took them, they went into the living room, sat on the couch, and started to drink. But as soon as she looked at Ricky, Pearl started smiling again, and she smiled and smiled and smiled.

"Why are you smiling like that?" asked Ricky. "Stop it."

"I can't help it," she said. As if to demonstrate, she tried for a moment not to smile, but she couldn't do it. Grinning from ear to ear, she gave a helpless shrug.

Ricky stared. "You are glowing," he said. "When you are happy, you glow."

Pearl blushed and shrugged again, the grin still plastered across her face. Ricky couldn't take his eyes off her.

"I'll be back soon," he said. "In May."

"I know. May 5th."

"Yes," he said.

And then there didn't seem much else to say. Ricky picked up a cookie, tasted it, and put it down. Pearl watched him, and her smile gradually faded.

"How long do you have in Ottawa," she asked, "before your next fundraising tour?"

"Three weeks."

"Are you looking forward to it?"

Ricky shrugged. "I don't know," he said. "It'll be nice, at least, to be in my own place, and not in a hotel."

"Plus you'll get to see your friends," said Pearl.

Ricky turned and looked at her directly. "I don't have friends," he said. "Or anyway, no one...like you—" And he looked suddenly so stricken and forlorn that Pearl laughed—kindly, lovingly.

"It's all right," she said. "It's only ten weeks."

Dumbly he nodded.

Pearl threw her arms around him, and held him to her gently. With her thumb she stroked the back of his neck, once, twice, thrice, thinking in big bold words, like the words that swam in her dream: *I love you. I love you. I love you.* Then slowly she let go of him.

When they were separate again, Ricky said:

"Before—when I wanted to—I didn't mean—I didn't mean to rush us—"

"I know," said Pearl. And for the second time that evening, she gave him back his own words. "It's okay. We have time. We have all the time in the world."

Ricky nodded, but he seemed distracted.

"Time..." he said, and looked down at his watch. "Oh Christ!" he cried, leaping to his feet. "It's nearly 7:15. I'm going to miss my plane!"

Pearl stood up and followed Ricky as he strode to the vestibule, pulled on his boots, snatched his coat from the closet and yanked it on. He turned to Pearl. For a brief moment, he looked at her tenderly. Then he grabbed her, gave her a long, deep kiss, and without looking at her again, turned and walked out the door. From the doorway Pearl watched him hurry down the steps. It was extremely dark out, she was surprised by the darkness, it had been dark when he arrived, but not like this, not this deep darkness. Then she noticed that the streetlamp across the road was broken—that explained it. It was so dark now that Ricky seemed to disappear the second he reached the end of her walkway. As if he had fallen off the end of the earth, or never really been. But to her right, on the big square of lawn between her house and Auntie Dorothy's, the snow glistened a luminous and surreal blue: a glowing, frozen garden electrified under the moon.

~
179

Part Four

There is silence. Pearl has stopped talking. I wait, thinking she is going to go on, but she just sits there, looking down. I have become entranced by her voice and its rhythms, and the sudden halt to it is strange, almost shocking.

"Wow," I say into the silence, "this is amazing." My voice feels rusty, and it sounds thicker than usual, like the first words spoken after a deep night's sleep.

"You didn't know?" asks Pearl, looking up.

"How would I know?" I ask, and then guiltily think of Auntie Bella, and how she usually told me everything.

"My mother...?"

"No," I say, "she didn't say a word."

Pearl is studying me closely.

"She didn't," I say.

"I made her swear," says Pearl. "I said if she told anyone..."

"Well, she stuck to it," I say. "She didn't breathe a word. Not to me, anyway."

We are silent for a while. Pearl looks down. She brushes something off her knee.

"I knew you'd understand," she says. "You've always liked"— she looks at me carefully—"*boys*." She blushes slightly. "Sex. All that." I look back steadily. "I never did," she says. "I kept thinking when I was with Ricky, 'Eve would understand about this. Eve knows all about these things.'"

A little embarrassed, I shrug. Then I say, "It's wonderful, anyway, you discovering all this."

Pearl doesn't say anything, she's drifting off again.

"Well, go on," I say impatiently. "What happened then? What happened when he came back in May?"

"You're not bored?" asks Pearl. "This isn't boring? You have time?"

"Bored? Why would I be bored? Go on...What happened next?"

The following day, Pearl's mother came back from her trip, full of complaints and pictures and presents.

"What did you buy this for?" asked Pearl, lifting out of Bella's open suitcase a lacy, black shawl and holding it up to view. "I don't know...I just liked it," said Bella. Pearl didn't say anything; but when her mother paused in her unpacking to go to the bathroom, Pearl grabbed the shawl and ran upstairs. Draping it around her, she danced round and round her room. When she got tired of dancing, she wrapped the shawl tightly around her like a fishnet cocoon, and sat in it on her bed.

On the outside, nothing much changed in her life. She passed her days in her room the same way she had passed them before. But now she was no longer alone. She talked with Ricky from the moment she woke up in the morning until she fell asleep at night. Her first thought on waking, the first word on her lips, was *Ricky*. She shared everything with him, from her little in-jokes and insights to the tired aching in her body; and when they watched T.V. together, the soap operas soaped her desire for him. Nightly she wanted him, and often during the day too, and he made love to her whenever she wanted, the way he had when they were together—gently, passionately—but this time to completion, consummating their unconsummated love. There was nothing they didn't share. He even followed her into the bathroom and watched her brush her teeth; and with him there, even this most mundane act became transformed by the joy of intimacy. Ricky loved the way she brushed her teeth, it made him laugh. "Typical," he said, as he watched her brush systematically, first all the upper teeth on the outside, then the bottom outside, then the upper inside, and the lower inside. She checked how it looked, rinsed and spat, and looked up at him. He smiled back. Everything about her was all right, was okay, because it was loved. He even watched her, loving her, when she was curled up in a ball on her bed, filled with terror, anxiety, and dread, that nameless thing that happened to her regularly every few days. She held tightly on to her hair, and rocked back and forth, back and forth. And he didn't laugh at her, he didn't call her stupid. He reached down and stroked her hair, and her forehead, and her cheek, and she stopped rocking, and the feeling went.

He also persuaded her to eat. The third time they'd sat together on the sofa, Ricky touched Pearl's thin, gauzy shirt where it swelled over her breasts, and ran his fingers down over her ribs, bump bump bump over each one of them, like speed bumps slowing him down. Then he paused and said, "Gotta put some meat on those bones," before bending down and kissing her on the belly-button where her shirt had ridden up, and on the zipper of her jeans, and the inside of her denim-covered thigh. So now Pearl ate chicken legs (or *polkas*, as her mother called them), and potato chips, and potato salad, and rolls still warm from the oven, and salad with vinaigrette dressing, and chocolate eclairs. And once when her mother was out, she tasted some Amaretto from the liquor cabinet—afterwards washing out her glass, drying it, and stealthily putting it away.

Not that she ate a thing in front of her mother. She wouldn't give her the satisfaction. But repeatedly Bella reached for a box of crackers and found it mysteriously, absurdly light, and inside, when she opened it, there was only a single broken cracker at the bottom. The same thing with her *mun* cookies, or when she went to the fridge, with the orange juice, the butterscotch pudding, and the sardine salad: just one token drop, spoonful, or smear was left behind. She didn't say a word to Pearl, being too smart, or too scared, or both. But she began cooking double, as if now there were really two people in the house, just like she used to cook when Uncle Harry was still alive. To Auntie Dorothy she squealed with delight, "She's eating! She's eating!" and she reported to her several times a day in minute detail: "For breakfast she had cereal and two crackers and juice." (She checked after each meal, like a detective, when Pearl was back up in her room.) "For lunch, spaghetti and salad, four cookies and a plum; for supper, chicken and chips; and for a midnight snack, a sardine sandwich and a cup of cocoa." Pearl's face began to fill out and so did her body. She was slim now rather than skinny. She had enough flesh covering her, you didn't feel pained when you looked at her. Her hair grew out, too.

But about five weeks after Ricky's visit, Pearl couldn't hear his voice any more, she couldn't recall his face either, and she began to wonder if any of what she remembered had ever really happened. She knew he wouldn't call or write. He had said so. "I don't write," he'd said, as if he was proud of it, as if it was a mark of his uniqueness, the way some people proudly say, "I never got past grade six." But she started to feel shaky, she wondered if this thing was real, and if he was right now thinking of her, and missing her, the way she was thinking about and missing him. For about eight days she vacillated—should she, shouldn't she, should she, shouldn't she?—each day putting it off till the next—until one day, when Bella was out, Pearl finally went to the old black wall-phone in the kitchen, and called up CARE to find out when in May, when exactly in May, Ricky Kessler would be coming to Montreal to speak on animal rights. And they did not say to her, "Ricky Kessler? We've never heard of him," or "There is no one here by that name, you must have a wrong number," or "He is a figment of your imagination." They told her he was coming from May 5th to 8th, and there would be numerous opportunities to meet the Director and hear what he had to say.

"May we put you on our mailing list?" the woman on the phone asked her; and Pearl in a happy haze said, "Sure," and gave out her name and address.

Four days later, Pearl received a big brown envelope saying

"CARE" on the front, and inside, among a treasure trove of pamphlets and brochures, was a letter to her, signed by Ricky, welcoming her into the CARE family. *So* this *was his handwriting!* and she traced the letters of his name with her index finger, one letter at a time, like a schoolgirl. Then she examined the rest of the materials. A green pamphlet describing the work of the organization: *"CARE is a not-for-profit advocacy group whose aim is to protect, promote and advance the rights, the health, and the welfare of all living creatures..."* A brochure with the "personal stories" of various animals, accompanied by their pictures: neglected and abused dogs, and cats, monkeys and birds. "You wouldn't treat a dog like this," said the caption under a spaniel with a black eye. And finally, a solicitation letter full of phrases underlined in blue pen, with a return envelope in the shape of a dog. Down the left-hand side of this letter, there were twenty or twenty-five names in very small print; and sitting at the top, of course, like a king over his subjects, was *"Ricky Kessler, Director,"* in bold. Seeing his name there, it hit Pearl, with a shock, that Ricky was alive, he was real. He wasn't just inside her, he was in the world, the real world; and anyone who wanted to could go up to him and touch him, anybody who wanted to could talk to him. And she was as appalled and embarrassed as if her innermost self, her pulpy, unprotected, private parts were suddenly on public display. She began to sweat. She grabbed at a brochure, as if for help, and opened it. Inside was a story about chemical testing on animals, and a photo of hair spray being sprayed directly into the eyes of a rabbit, causing immediate blindness.

"This is outrageous!" cried Pearl, showing it to Bella, demanding that she read it, every single word of it. She also insisted that Bella send in a cheque, right away, walk out right now to the corner on this miserable drizzly day, and mail it—now, now, *now.* Which

Bella, laughing nervously, did. As docile as a battered animal, she walked slowly there and back, painfully on her arthritic legs.

A few weeks later, in April, Pearl received another mailing from CARE, this time containing their annual report, twelve glossy pages, hot-off-the-press. Inside there was a summary of CARE's activities for the year, a list of all the donors who had contributed $250 or more, and some reproductions of newspaper clippings (one headline from the *Ottawa Herald* read *"CARE CARES"*). There were also three postcards, written by Ricky, just sign and send to your local M.P.: *"I am firmly opposed to the use of animals for testing cosmetic or other industrial products"*; and finally, of course, a thank-you note for her mother's donation, and a tax-deductible receipt for $25.

It was two weeks after that, however—on May 1st—that Pearl received what she'd really been waiting for: the spring newsletter, with page one announcing all the dates and times and locations where Ricky would be speaking in Montreal in honour of Save-the-Animals Month. "Feel free to come to as few or as many as you wish: lunchtime talks, parlour meetings in people's homes, a late-afternoon reception at The Montreal Club, breakfasts, dinners; and in between, the Director is available to meet the public and the press at the CARE office, by appointment only."

Filled with joy, Pearl read and reread Ricky's schedule, as if reading her own life. She kissed the page and hugged it to her chest. She danced around the room. Then, laughing, she sat down on the bed to read the rest of the newsletter. She turned the page, and there before her was a picture of Ricky with his arm around a woman with long blond hair, the two of them holding up a placard: "Animal Rights and Animal Wrongs: Stop Chemical Testing On Rabbits!" Underneath the picture, the caption read: "CARE Director Ricky Kessler and his Executive Assistant Micheline

Dubois protest last month in front of the Parliament buildings in Ottawa." Pearl looked again at the picture. Ricky was wearing a white turtleneck under a casual, stylish jacket, a pair of beige slacks, and loafers with white socks. Micheline was in an old-fashioned white blouse with lace at the collar and the wrists, and over it a black wool vest; a long brown hippie skirt with geometric shapes stencilled on it in black; and brown, pointy boots with buttons, like a witch might wear, standing on the snow-tipped grass. Pearl frowned, trying to see the relationship between the two of them. Ricky was looking straight ahead. But Micheline was looking toward Ricky, and she was not just smiling, she was laughing. Was he tickling her back, or her neck, to make her smile for the picture? And after it was taken, what did they do? Did she scoop up some snow from the grass and throw it at him in that feminine way—missing his face, of course, but grazing it, just enough to taunt and tempt him? Then he chased her, and caught her, and pulled her down, rolling with her into the snow. He looked down into her non-Jewish face, and grew serious; a longing came into her eyes, and he kissed her on the mouth. The rights of animals. The wrongs of animals. Animal rights, animal wrongs.

Nonsense. She, Pearl, was his oasis. His quiet glade. She knew this was true, he had said so. So why this pounding in her heart? Why was she suddenly dizzy and short of breath? Why was she panting, and clutching her hand to her chest like an old woman, like her mother? She longed to tear this picture up into a million tiny pieces and throw them into the garbage, so that none of this could ever have happened, so that he would never have put his arm around that long-legged, long-haired girl. But she could not do it. She could not tear up his face, the same way that religious Jews cannot tear up a piece of paper which has written upon it the name of God. For a long time Pearl stared at the photo. Then she went to her desk, took a pair of scissors from the drawer, and calmly, deliberately cut Micheline out of the picture. She started from the bottom right, from her boot, and went up her skirt and arm, around her shoulder and hair, over her head, and down her other shoulder (here cutting through Ricky's arm, the one that was draped around her, there was no choice but to cut it off). She continued down the other side, and underneath the two boots, literally cutting the ground out from under her.

She was gone.

But still this didn't achieve Pearl's purpose. The hole in the middle of the photo, a hole in the shape of a woman, actually highlighted, rather than diminished, Micheline's importance. It made Ricky look like Adam minus his Eve. Pearl hesitated a moment. Then she cut out the background of the picture, letting the sun, the sky, the placard, the snowy grass, and the rest of the newsletter, fall to the floor. What was left in her hand was a funny, unreal-looking Ricky, like the grown-ups she used to cut out from magazines in elementary school to stick into her scrapbooks. Ricky looked two-dimensional now, as people often do when you cut away their contexts. Spindly, and not altogether real.

In only two more weeks she would see him. And then she would ask him about the picture in the newsletter. She would not shout at him, she would not tear at her hair or pound on his chest with her fists. With dignity she would ask him to explain this photo, to explain himself. And he would. He would say that Micheline meant nothing to him, nothing to him at all; she was his secretary and nothing more. "How could you be so foolish?" he would ask. "How could you doubt me, how could you doubt our love for each other? Don't you realize I've never felt this way about anyone else before?" And he would bend down and look into her eyes, and kiss her. And everything would be exactly the same as it was.

Ricky's visit approached: one-and-a-half weeks away, then one week, then four days. Pearl got more and more excited and nervous. She couldn't remember him very well any more, but she knew that she loved him. Of this she was sure. Ten times a day she went to her closet, and from the middle shelf, from under her underwear, she took out the picture of Ricky. She stared at it, and talked to it, and even kissed it sometimes, just like the paper dolls she'd played with as a girl.

She didn't think about Micheline. But two days before Ricky's arrival, she said to an astonished Bella, "Let's go shopping. I'm tired of always wearing the same old clothes." So together they went off to see Henny Wolfson, a childhood friend of her mother's who sold designer clothes out of her basement, half price, with the labels cut off. Henny clucked and cooed over Pearl, who— after much hesitating, after being told over and over again that no, she didn't look fat, she looked absolutely lovely—finally agreed to a single outfit: a soft, pink turtleneck sweater and a long, pink and grey skirt, with a pair of small silver earrings in the shape of a rose.

The night before Ricky arrived, Pearl got herself ready. The new outfit hung from the top of her closet door, covering the poster of the little Biafra girl. Pearl stroked the soft sweater. She held the earrings up to her ears in front of the mirror. She ran a hot bubble bath scented with strawberries, and gingerly stepped in.

In the bath, she opened herself, she opened her body. And as soon as she did, she felt her own nakedness—the terror, but also the thrill, of leaving herself so wide-open, so vulnerable, to another person. The next day she would hold nothing back from Ricky. (Why should she? He already knew everything about her, and he loved her; there was nothing she needed to hide.) She wanted to be completely naked with him—completely open and undefended— so that they could be naked together, so they could be as intimate as two bodies, two souls, could be. Pearl lay in the bathtub, letting her layers, her coverings, her defenses melt away, like so much dirt and dead skin. And when she was done, even the silken bathwater felt rough to her: The strawberry bubbles breaking against her belly and breasts and back were like hundreds of minute acid explosions against her raw and tender flesh. She'd made herself ready for love.

⋆━◉━⋆

The next morning, Pearl woke up early, put on her new outfit, sat on her bed, and waited.

But Ricky didn't call.

Not that day.

And not the next day.

And not the day after that, either.

By Sunday morning, Pearl was no longer waiting. She was stunned. She lay on her bed, numb, frozen, feeling nothing. She wasn't waiting, any more than a hibernating animal is waiting for spring; it's simply sleeping until the time comes for it to wake up. And as if in a long, hibernating dream, Pearl made excuses for Ricky: He was probably terribly busy, with everyone wanting to meet him, everyone grabbing at him—donors, the media, his staff...He had breakfasts, and luncheons, and dinners, and meetings every minute in-between. She was sure he hadn't had the tiniest oasis for himself, or else he would have called by now, at least to say hello and plan when they could meet. It didn't mean anything that he hadn't yet called. Sometime during the day he would—he wasn't leaving till eleven that night (there was a 7:30 dinner, his final event). He would call, and they would see each other, and then this strange, unreal dream would be over.

But when 2:30 rolled around, and then 3:00, the impossible seemed to be happening. He was not calling. Pearl couldn't believe it. It was not possible that he wouldn't call. He loved her. He had never met anyone like her before. He had said so. He had told her that this was "different, this was meaningful." He'd said to her, "Look at you, how beautiful you are..." He'd kissed her all over her face; and then all over her body: on her hands, and her breasts, and her thighs, and her belly. He loved her. She knew he did.

At 3:25, the phone finally rang. Pearl leaped off the bed, ran to the kitchen, and grabbed the phone.

"Hello?" she said breathlessly.

"Hello?" said a man's voice.

"Hello?" said Pearl, her heart pounding.

"Yes."

"Ricky?"

"What?"

"Ricky, is that you?"

"This is the butcher—Yankel Meirovitch Fine Meats. Is this Mrs. Hirschman?"

The butcher?

"Mrs. Hirschman, are you there? Hallo? Mrs. Hirschman?"

Bella came up beside Pearl. "Who is it?" she asked.

Dumbly Pearl handed her the phone, and went upstairs. She sat on her bed. Dazed. For about an hour and a half she stared blankly straight ahead, biting on her knuckle.

It's not possible. It's not possible...

At 5:45, Pearl got up to go to the bathroom. She left her room and started down the hall, when she saw her mother from the back, waddling toward the bathroom, pill bottle in hand, to take her medication. Pearl was suddenly filled with rage, and pounced on her.

"What are you taking those pills for?" she yelled. "I told you, you don't need them. There's nothing wrong with you. You just use them as a crutch. I'm going to throw them out—yes, I am, I'm going to throw them all out, once and for all!"

"No, Pearl, no," protested Bella.

"Yes. Yes, I am..."

Pearl tried to grab the pills from her, but Bella resisted. They struggled, they fought, and after about a minute, Pearl wrestled the bottle away from her. Quickly she unscrewed the top, turned the bottle upside down, and in a white cascade, flushed all the pills down the toilet. Bella was sobbing and wringing her hands. "I need them, Pearl, I need them. What am I going to do now? Today is Sunday, the drug store's closed..."

"I don't care," snarled Pearl. "Die if you need to." She stomped off to her room and slammed the door.

Her chest heaving, Pearl lay on her bed. Bella's sobbing gradually died down. Outside night was falling. Without looking at the clock, Pearl knew it was exactly 6:21. Soon it would be time for Ricky to go to his dinner...

How could he not have called yet? It was simply not possible. It wasn't possible that he could be here, ten minutes away from her house, and not call her. If he were here, he would have called. Maybe he never got here. Maybe he never got to Montreal. What if he'd gotten sick? What if on the way he'd gotten into an accident, and was right now lying somewhere in a pool of blood, bleeding to death? Or flat on his back in a hospital bed, with tubes coming out of his arms, nose and mouth? How could she have so misjudged him? How could she have mistrusted him? He was probably not even here. He probably never even got to Montreal.

Her worry for him, her love, moved her where all her own need could not. She rose from her bed, barefoot, in a cotton nightgown—like a sleepwalker, a Lady Macbeth—and made her way down the stairs, along the cold floor of the hallway, and into the kitchen. She picked up the phone, and dialed the number by heart.

"Is Ricky Kessler there?" she asked.

"Speaking," said the voice at the other end.

He's here. He's here...

"Ricky!" she said. "It's Pearl."

There was a pause. She felt his surprise, she felt him collecting himself. Then he rose to the occasion. His voice was measured and cordial.

"Pearl!" he said. "How nice to hear from you."

"Yes," said Pearl. And that was all she could think of to say. She was all of a sudden underwater, deep at the bottom of the ocean, and waiting like a grain of sand to feel the warmth of his love.

There was a pause.

"How are you?" she asked.

"Fine," he said. "Busy."

There was another pause.

"And you?" he asked.

"Fine," she said weakly, feeling the strength seep out of her. There was no warmth in his voice, there was nothing coming from him at all, there was nothing there. Even anger, "Why are you calling me?" might have been better, easier to bear, than this cool courtesy, this dealing with her in businesslike mode, as though she were just another CARE member calling him up.

"How long are you here for?" asked Pearl. But in her fear, she'd whispered it, it had spoken itself almost entirely inside her, travelling from so deep in her heart it only made it to the inner frontier of her skin.

"What?" he asked.

She repeated her question more loudly.

"Oh, I'm leaving tonight," he said. "In a couple of hours."

There was a pause. Then he said a little more warmly, "I thought of calling you, you know. It was...great meeting you last time I was here. But this trip has been absolutely mad. You can't imagine what it's been like. They've barely given me time to eat."

There was silence. Then Pearl whispered something.

"What?" asked Ricky.

"I said"—and she felt like she was shouting, it took the effort of a shout to make her words rise to the surface of her body, and come out, to get somehow past her lips—"Maybe next time you're here, we could meet."

"Oh, sure," he said, sounding relieved. "Sure, that would be nice—look, I gotta go now...I'm sorry. There's someone waiting for me."

"Oh. Okay."

"Listen," said Ricky, and he paused for a moment. "I'm sorry."

Pearl nodded, forgetting that he couldn't see her. Pain was starting to fill her, beginning in her stomach—a quickly spreading warmth, like a burn...

"Bye," he said.

"Bye."

Slowly Pearl hung up the phone. Slowly, sleepwalking, she made her way back up the stairs. *This has been a dream, this is nothing but a dream.* The house was very quiet, utterly silent—maybe her mother was sleeping, maybe she was dead. Pearl continued slowly to her room. She went in and shut the door. She lay on her bed, her arm flung over her face.

This had not been Ricky. This had not been her Ricky. This was an impostor, someone trained to sound like him. An impersonator. Someone playing a joke:

He's sorry, but he's very busy. He's gotta go. Someone's waiting for him.

Her Ricky would never have said that. Her Ricky was going to take her away. He was going to take her to Vancouver. They were going to have babies. A house. A life...

She started to cry. Which made no sense. Because she didn't

believe that this conversation was real. But her body did. Her eyes were crying. And that pain in her belly that had started when she was on the phone was expanding—getting bigger and bigger by the second. It was a slow burn, an electrical burn, neither hot nor cold, just a current of pain running between her vagina and her heart, and filling in everything in-between. The whole area was vibrating, throbbing, aching. Then the pain began to increase in fierceness and intensity, as though someone were slowly turning up a dial—and it got worse and worse, until Pearl was sure her insides were going to explode. She couldn't endure this pain. It was burning her. Her body was being burnt.

And just then, in the middle of this pain, exactly in the middle of it—if this were a hurricane, right where the eye would be—a hole appeared. A teeny hole, no larger than a pinprick, like the kind punched into cardboard in the very first cameras for the eye to look through. And out of this pinprick hole, came some words, whispering:

"He doesn't love you. He doesn't love you."

The voice that was saying this was not a cruel voice. It was quiet and matter-of-fact, potentially helpful even, like a vaccination—a small, gentle dose of something dangerous, even deadly, to strengthen you against larger doses to come. If she could take in this little bit now, the pain would be less later on. But she couldn't. She couldn't absorb that Ricky didn't love her, any more than she could have absorbed the statement, "You are dead." You couldn't be dead and be hearing someone say that to you. Similarly, if Ricky didn't love her, she'd die. And she was not dead. She was perfectly all right. Although she was dizzy suddenly, everything was spinning around. It was hot. And she couldn't breathe.

She passed out, thinking she was falling down a well.

She slept for a bit. But there was no escaping: She woke, and before she could block it out, before she could remember not to remember, the pain was back, searing through her body—as if she'd been given an IV injection of hot French mustard made into a liquid, introduced into her body directly through a vein. Scalding it, and within a matter of seconds scalding the inside of every other vein in her body. In her arms, her legs, through her torso, her head. Not an inch of her was safe from it. She was filled to the brim, like a *kiddish* cup, with pain.

She screamed. (A muffled scream—face down into her pillow, so her mother wouldn't hear.) Then she turned over, pulled the pillow tightly over her face, and screamed again. And again. And again. And again.

Most of all it hurt in those soft, open places, the places Ricky had opened in her, the places he himself had softened. Everywhere he'd kissed her, everywhere she'd wanted to be kissed, these were now places only of pain. He'd opened every pore in her, every duct of feeling, only to pour into them black, burning tar. As dark and deadly as liquid hate.

She fell asleep again, exhausted by pain.

She woke up an hour and a half later, drenched in sweat, and aching. She realized immediately that she was sick. She was filled with a great heaviness and a dullness. Indifferently she thought that maybe she was going to die. It was dark out now, it was 9:27, and she could hear her mother moving around. She dozed off again...

She slept till dawn. This time when she woke up, it was just like it had been all the mornings during the sixty-nine days that she and Ricky were apart. She woke to find his hand on her breast, and his face right in front of hers, smiling at her tenderly.

Everything's okay now. It was all just a dream. He loves me...

And then the vision was gone.

And that vaccination voice returned, less gentle this time:

He doesn't love you.

He doesn't love you.

He doesn't love you.

It continued, and it was like being kicked—over and over again—in the stomach:

He doesn't love you. He doesn't love you. He doesn't love you.

"Stop it!" cried Pearl. "Yes he does!"

Of course he doesn't, the voice said reasonably, and now this voice sounded familiar, vaguely she recognized it, though she couldn't say exactly from where:

How could he?

Why would he?

Someone like him, someone like you.

Why would he choose you?

You're fucked-up.

You're frightened, you're ugly, you're a crazy person.

You're a recluse who bites your knuckle all day long.

Why should he love you?

No one will ever love you.

Ever.

The pain that tore through her now was like a raging, wild animal clawing at her entrails. It wanted to destroy her, she didn't stand a chance against it...

And in an instant, like a genie doing its disappearing act, Pearl was back underwater again—floating, and alone, far away from savage animals and voices. She was floating like a fish, or a letter, or a letter-fish, or some other strange hybrid form of life that hasn't been invented yet. Something that nowadays, in our time, is seen as mutant, but that in a hundred, or two hundred years, when there are many more like her around, might be taken, along with everything else, as just another species in the world.

She curled up in her warm ocean, underwater, underwater where no one could reach her. With her right hand, she grasped her own hair—or was it seaweed? Or a snake? A cold current came by, and ran through her, and was gone—

She floated. She floated...

⊷═◉═⊶

For the rest of that day, Pearl slept, and woke, suffered, and slept. Woke again, suffered again, slept again. And on and on. And this day, as agonizing as the night that preceded it, was repeated over and over again, ten, twenty, thirty times. Pearl simply couldn't believe that Ricky didn't love her. It seemed to be obvious, there was no escaping the facts. But she just couldn't believe it. She couldn't take it in. Her nights were tortured, her days were tortured, day and night blurred together, and time lost all meaning. Weeks went by and she didn't notice their passing; a single hour could feel to her like a fortnight.

She did what she could to protect herself. She tried not to think about Ricky; but it was impossible. She had nothing else to think about but him, he had become the centre of her world, and all thoughts flowed toward him as naturally, as inevitably, as a river flowing to the sea. She had gotten into the habit of talking to him constantly, sharing everything with him. And of conjuring up his face whenever she needed to feel loved, or beautiful, thinking happily to herself: *He loves my cheek. He loves my eyes. He loves my nose. He loves my mouth. He loves this shoulder. And this breast. And this freckle on my breast...* She tried not to think about this now, but she couldn't help it. And then, suddenly, it turned on her. It became instead: *He doesn't love these eyes any more. Or this cheek. Or this mouth. Or this nose. This is an elbow that Ricky doesn't love. This is a thigh that he doesn't love. Ugly face. Stupid ugly elbow. Fat, disgusting thigh.* Her body became repulsive to her, because Ricky no longer loved it. And if he no longer loved it, it was no longer lovable. It was something to be detested. And she detested it.

And not only her body—herself. She was filled with rage—not at Ricky, of course (he was all love, he was all beauty)—but at her own hideousness, worthlessness, stupidity. That voice had been right. How could she ever have thought that he might love her? No one could love somebody as despicable, disgusting, as unlovable as her—except maybe a criminal, a murderer, a serial killer—the only kind of person in the world who wasn't too good for her. But someone like Ricky— normal, handsome, successful—how could she ever have thought...?

She started hurting herself, scratching at her body until she drew blood, and it felt good to do this, it gave her pleasure, it was what she deserved. She began in the bend of her left arm, where she had had eczema as a child and where it used to itch all the time. Then she scratched the rest of that arm, and then the other arm. And soon she was tearing at herself all over: at her legs, and her neck, and her breasts, and her stomach. She stripped off her clothes and clawed at herself, as if trying to get underneath to another, inner skin where her feelings were buried. So that she could feel something in her body again. Because she couldn't feel anything there any more. All the feeling was gone. But it wasn't like it had been before she met Ricky, when she was like this all the time. Because then she hadn't known that anything was missing, she hadn't known what it was like to be alive. And now she knew.

Tell him to come back. He has to come back. He has taken away all the feeling—all the happiness and pleasure—in her body, and he must give it back. She loaned it to him, she only loaned it to him, on trust. He must come over at least one more time, and return it. Like a borrowed coat. (Surely no one would borrow a coat and then just not give it back. Not someone like him: an honest person, a decent person, not a common thief.) And she needed it. She needed it to be herself again, her new-found, wonderful self. There was a piece of her that was missing now.

And as if to demonstrate this visually, starting thirty days after the phone call, about a third of Pearl's body quickly disappeared. Within a week she lost all the weight she had put on for Ricky, returning to the weight she was when they first met. In two more weeks, she lost another fifteen pounds. And two weeks after that, fifteen more. The flesh melted off her. Her weight, which had been well below normal to start with, dropped lower and lower until she was almost skin and bones. She ate virtually nothing: at most a slice of bread a day, and often not even that; and when she was thirsty, she merely touched a little water to her lips. That was all that millions of people in the world had to live on, she told Bella, and why should she think herself better than them? As she said this, she looked nearly skeletal; and Bella, frantic, desperate, half-hysterical, began screaming at her, begging her, "But you have to eat! You have to! Pearl! Please! Eat something! Tell me what you want. I'll make you anything you want..."

Twice that month Pearl was rushed to the hospital, after crumpling on the floor at the bottom of the stairs.

"Dizziness. Malnutrition," said the father knows best–type doctor. And he put her on intravenous: a glutinous, life-giving substance flowing against her will into her veins.

But they couldn't keep her there forever; and once home, she almost immediately lost whatever strength she'd built up. She just got weaker and weaker, and thinner and thinner, looking more each day like the girl in the poster.

Only ten weeks had passed since Pearl called Ricky, and inside her now there was nothing but empty silence. As if the person who had lived in there, who had walked, and talked, and gestured with her hands, had simply moved out. Because below a certain weight, you feel nothing. Something dies—just as below a certain soil temperature, no plant can possibly live. Pearl stopped getting her period, her body shut down.

She was dying.

⊷⊶

One day, Bella overslept. Pearl came downstairs at around ten o'clock, disturbed by the silence in the house, and there she saw, lying on the floor of the vestibule—pushed through the slot in the door by the postman—a big, brown envelope from CARE. Pearl had instructed Bella, of course, to go through the mail every morning, and throw out anything that arrived from CARE, which she diligently did, being an early riser anyway, and always being finished with this task well before Pearl woke up. But today she slept late, and for the first time in fourteen weeks, Pearl saw a letter from CARE. The envelope had a new symbol on it now: instead of a spaniel, a Doberman pinscher. A handsome but savage dog. The one used by the Nazis.

For a while Pearl stood staring at the envelope, as if it were a dog that might bite. Then she went over and gingerly picked it up. She took it into the living room, sat down with it on the old green couch, and opened it on her lap. Inside she found the fall newsletter, with a list of upcoming events on the first page, and a report from the Director on the second. Ricky's four days in Montreal were mentioned as one of the highlights of the past few months, thanks to the half-a-million-dollar grant that he managed, while there, to secure from The Montreal Foundation.

Pearl flipped a couple of pages, and there suddenly before her was a picture of Ricky's face. He looked totally real: He was looking straight in front of him, straight at her. He was smiling slightly, and his eyes were warm. Her stomach immediately contracted, that mustard pain flashing through it, in and out in a moment. He was looking right at her, he was telling her something. He was telling her that everything was all right. No, he wasn't going to come back and marry her. But yes, he'd loved her when they were together. Yes, what had happened between them was real. He hadn't been using her, it wasn't just a fling for him. On the contrary—it had frightened him, and afterwards he hadn't known how to handle it. He should have called her when he came to Montreal in May, he was sincerely sorry about that. But anyway she shouldn't doubt what had happened between them. He'd loved her. He had. And in a way he still did.

Pearl was looking at him with disbelieving joy; and was just trying to think how to answer him, when all of a sudden he was gone. The realness disappeared from the picture, and Pearl found herself holding, and preparing to talk to, a black-and-white photo, as though it were a real person. It was just a piece of paper, with an image on it captured by a camera. Slowly she put the newsletter back into her lap.

She sat for a moment. Then she got up and went into the kitchen. Carefully she folded the newsletter in half, and put it behind the cookie jar with the other important papers. Then she took a slice of bread from the pantry. She spread it with margarine. She ate it.

And from that point on, from then till now, she has been eating. Not a lot. But enough. She's let her body live.

Part Five

Pearl stops talking and looks at me. "That's it," she says with a shrug. She looks down at the bedspread, and plays for a bit with a loose thread. Then she looks up.

"I know that nothing is ever going to happen between me and Ricky," she says frankly. "I know that. But also I know that in his heart he still loves me. I know he does."

I don't answer; I just look at her. She is sitting right in front of me—cross-legged and comfortable in her cotton clothes, very much *Pearl*—and she is so close that I could lean forward, if I wanted, and touch her on the knee. And suddenly I grasp how near she came to not being here, sitting with me right now; how her life, for a while, hung by an ever-thinning thread; and how close I was to losing her, without even knowing it. I look now into her face, and see also, with a shock, that the story isn't over—not at all. She is still terribly fragile and thin, and the scale could at any moment tip back the other way. The smallest thing could do it. Not to mention the largest—guiltily I remember Auntie Bella, and wonder if over the past two days Pearl has eaten anything at all. To look at her you wouldn't think so. She is so thin that even her skin looks thin. It is translucent, you can see a faint light below the surface, and the fine tracings of blue veins. "You're too thin-skinned," Auntie Dorothy always told her, "you need to develop a thicker skin." But she can't; she was born this way. Feeling everything. There is no door, no barrier—what is outside, around her, is inside her, too. People walk right in, right through her skin. Ricky walked in; and now he sits cross-legged, and laughing, impish-evil as Rumpelstiltskin, right in the centre of her heart. She has no reverse door by which to usher out visitors who have hurt or abused her, or otherwise misbehaved. Once they're in, they're in, and they can torment her all they want, she is trapped with them forever.

"I know that nothing is ever going to happen," Pearl continues. "But I can't stop thinking about him anyway. I think about him all the time. Sometimes I think I must be crazy, thinking so much about something that I know I'm never going to have. But I can't help it. *You* know about men, Eve. Tell me how to get over him. Tell me how to not love him any more."

She asks me this with complete and utter confidence in my expert knowledge, the way she might ask a fireman how to put out a fire. But I don't feel knowledgeable at all. I haven't the faintest idea how to help her. My back hurts from sitting cross-legged for so long; I shift positions—I lean back against the wall and pull my knees up to my chest with my hands clasped in front. I don't know how to solve her problem; but one thing anyway seems clear to me now, and that is that Pearl is not crazy. She knows that it's over with Ricky, that he is never—for the rest of her life—going to call her again. She knows this is true, her mind clearly understands the situation. It's just that her body doesn't. Even now, one year later, it still wants Ricky the way a shoulder wants its amputated arm. Her breasts want his lips. Her thighs want his fingers. And all of her wants to feel his arms around her, holding her tight. Because Ricky's touch, his touch on her skin, is an imprint, like the imprinting of ducks, who for the rest of their lives love as their parent whomever they happen to see when they first open their eyes. (Human, animal, it doesn't matter.) Ricky's imprint upon her cannot be swept away, not after one year and not after forty; it is indelible, like the branding on a cow's hide or on a human arm— as if he had branded her, burned her with his name, or his number. Forty years from now she might bump into him again, and even if she hasn't thought of him in all that time—even if her mind has forgotten everything, and so has her heart—if as he is talking to her, he casually puts his hand on her arm, she will tremble, and remember. It will all come flooding back. How he touched her. Exactly. Because the body never forgets.

Pearl is looking at me expectantly, trustingly.

"I'm no big expert," I say. "But one thing I've found is, it helps to get angry. Even hate him a little, if you can." I am surprised by what just came out of my mouth, I have no idea where it came from. "Otherwise you'll never get over him," I end authoritatively, as though I know what I'm talking about.

"I can't believe it!" cries Pearl, and explains that she has just reached the same conclusion herself. "Isn't it funny?" she asks. "Back in the sixties, we thought that love was the answer to everything: *All you need is love, duh - duh duh duh duh...*" But lately, she explains, she thinks there are times when what you really need is hate. Like now, when her insides are as soft and vulnerable as mush, and she aches day after day, month after month, with hopeless, helpless longing. Hate, like anger, is sharp and hard, and you can defend yourself with it, defend yourself with it against love.

But it is hard to turn love into hate.

"I've tried," she tells me earnestly. "You can't imagine how I've tried. But I just can't seem to hate him. How can you hate someone, how can you be angry at them, when it's not their fault? That's what I can't figure out. He was only ten years old when his mother died. Can you imagine that? And he was such a sensitive person, it broke his heart. Here I am an adult, and...I don't know...I don't really believe—but anyway, it's different. He was just a little boy. In a way he's still just a broken little boy, whatever he looks like on the outside. How can you hate someone like that?"

"He's an asshole. He hurt you."

"He didn't mean to," says Pearl. "It wasn't his fault. Because of his mother, he's afraid of love..."

"Love, shmove," I say, and then stop. There's no point arguing with her. She can't afford to hate him: he's too much a part of her. It would be like shooting bullets at your own reflection in the mirror. No one can do that.

Pearl stares at me. Then she says, "I wish I were more like you. Stronger. You would never be in a position like this. You'd've been over him ages ago."

I shrug. "I don't know," I say. "Maybe I'm not as strong as you think."

For a moment Pearl looks at me piercingly. "I know that, actually," she says. "I remember how hurt you were by Bobby Zuker, when he dumped you for Judy Blasterman."

It hurts, her saying that. Even now. *Dumped you.* She didn't have to say *dumped you.*

"You remember that," I say.

"How could I forget?" asks Pearl. "He was your first boyfriend. But anyway, you know me, I remember everything. Remember how nobody could ever beat me at *Concentration*?" I think for a moment and nod. "But it's got a bad side, too," she says. "I never forget *any*thing. You do, though. You know how to forget. You keep things in their proper perspective. Somehow you *get on*," she says. "You have a family, you have a career..."

I have a family. I have a career.

Meet my husband Mike, eight years older than I, now with a middle-age paunch, standing at the kitchen counter with his back to me, making himself a bologna sandwich. (He always has his back to me, it seems—if it isn't work, then it's something else.) My two golden-haired daughters, twelve and fourteen, sit at the kitchen table, fighting over something or other, as usual. My younger son, the one who looks like me, is in his room, silently building Lego towers, aiming for the sky. The older one stomps around the house, hating his father with a passion. (I probably should take him to a psychologist, but I have so little faith...and who knows? Maybe he'll outgrow it.)

My career is being second-in-command at a family counselling centre in the basement of a hospital, an administrative job with a lot of paperwork and little in the way of interest or challenge. I'll never be number one there, doing the things I want, because the current director is an old fox who's been there forever and will never retire, or die. I spend my breaks standing around the broken water cooler, drinking stale, tepid water with stale, tepid people. And here I will be for the rest of my career, because in only twelve years, I am eligible for early retirement and a fabulous pension too good to refuse.

"Yes," I say drily to Pearl. "I *get on.*"

She looks at me closely. Curiously even. And her face is so open and guileless, that I suddenly feel a great rush of affection.

Smiling, I say to her, "If you want to know how to turn love into hate, I can tell you how to do it."

"How?" she asks.

"It's easy," I say. "Just marry the guy."

There's a pause. "That's not funny," says Pearl.

"It wasn't meant to be," I answer.

Pearl looks down for a moment, digesting this. Then she looks up at me. "I didn't know you and Mike were having problems," she says.

I shrug. "That's life," I say. "It's not all beer and skittles." (One of Auntie Bella's favourite expressions.)

Pearl nods appreciatively. There is silence for a bit. Then she says, "There must be a way, though. Someone must have figured this out by now. I can't be the first one in the world to be in this situation."

"Whoever does is gonna to make a fortune," I say.

Pearl doesn't say anything. She just sits there, looking sad, and I have never felt more stupid and useless in my life. I have a Ph.D. in abnormal psychology, and almost two decades of clinical experience, I have helped hundreds of people over the years with their problems, and yet I can't think of a single useful thing to say to my cousin.

"All I can think of," I say to Pearl, "is that stupid game we used to play as kids."

"Which game?"

"You know, the one where you switch the letters..."

Pearl looks at me blankly.

"You know," I say. "Where you switch one letter at a time—like, MOUSE, HOUSE, HORSE...you change the 'M' to an 'H'—"

"Oh yeah! I remember," says Pearl. "But why are you thinking now about *that*?"

"Well," I say, "it's one way to go from LOVE to HATE."

"Oh, I see," says Pearl. "With the letters, you mean."

"Yeah."

"Hmm," says Pearl. "It shouldn't be too hard. You could go from LOVE...to LAVE..."

I think for a second. "Or LOVE to HOVE," I say.

"HOVE? What's HOVE? There's no such word."

"HOVE," I say. "Like 'heave'. You know—'heave-ho'."

"'Heave-hove'. You're just making that up," says Pearl.

"No I'm not."

"You probably are. You always used to do that in Scrabble."

"I am not!" I say, laughing. "I swear. It's a real word."

"Oh, all right then," says Pearl. She gets up, grabs a pencil and notepad from her desk, sits back down again, and hands them to me. "You write," she says. "LOVE LAVE. And LOVE HOVE..."

Within a minute or two we've come up with three different ways to transform LOVE into HATE. There's LOVE-HOVE-HAVE-HATE. There's LOVE-LAVE-HAVE-HATE. And there's LOVE-LAVE-LATE-HATE. We are happy and proud of ourselves, Pearl and I, as if we have just solved one of the ancient mysteries of the world. We're laughing, and then our laughter subsides. The room gets quiet. Outside the window, dusk is falling. We sit for a while in silence.

Then Pearl looks me straight in the eye.

"Why doesn't he love me?" she asks. "*Really* love me, I mean. Tell me the truth—Is it me? Is it something about me...?"

I lower my eyes as if that will screen out her pain.

"I don't know," I say. And I really don't. I have no idea why Ricky doesn't love her. Why anybody falls in love with anybody else, or doesn't. Or why you can sometimes fall *in* love, and then *out* again, as quickly as an alleycat falling into a garbage can, and then jumping back out. I hardly ever have answers, it seems, but I always have questions: *Why? Why?* echoes in me all the time...Why, for instance, Ricky started up with her in the first place. He could've had anyone he wanted, a man like him: good-looking, successful...Why did he pick someone plain and quiet, unshiny and shy, like my cousin Pearl? Why did he say and do what he did when the two of them first met? Couldn't he see who he was dealing with, couldn't he tell from the outset what kind of a girl she was?

Of course he could. He was sophisticated and ambitious; and as instinctively as a wolf sizing up its surroundings for dangers and opportunities, Ricky must have sized up Pearl, and seen something in her that could be useful to him. But what? How could she possibly have been useful? She had no money, status, or connections, nothing of any value to him politically. Perhaps to boost his ego, his fragile self-esteem? Yet any one of a hundred other women would have done better for that. Women more sophisticated, stylish, and successful than Pearl. High-heeled lawyers in their tailored suits and pearls. Or a Westmount princess looking for a prince. Why come back to Pearl seven days in a row? And tell her that she's like his innermost soul? Why? Why bother? When he could've been picking up women, hobnobbing at The Montreal Club?

There is no reasonable answer. Except one—and it catches me totally off guard, like the atheist who set out to prove the non-existence of God, and after compiling all the evidence, suddenly found he had proved the opposite. Ricky loved her. He must have. He probably even loved her as much as she thought he did, she wasn't imagining it at all. But if this is true, it's also most likely that he fell in love with her in spite of himself, he hadn't really wanted to, he hadn't ever intended to get deeply involved with another human being. He couldn't help it, though—something in her called out to him.

And now I start seeing things from Ricky's point of view; and maybe Pearl was right, actually, that what happened wasn't entirely his fault. How could he have known, after all, that he was dealing with a 41-year-old virgin? Maybe even a 4-year-old, or a 1-year-old (a frightened infant alone in its crib). Now I feel as if I am back at work, listening to a bickering couple, seeing both sides, and being (as always) the impartial, non-judgmental judge, the one who understands—and accepts—everything and everybody. But goddamit, I am not a psychologist here, mediating a marital conflict, and Pearl is not my client. She is my cousin, my flesh and blood. My blood-sister, with whom I swapped blood the summer I was ten, pricking our index fingers with a black-tipped needle we'd sterilized with a match, watching the two little balls of blood bubble up on our fingerpads, and rubbing them together so we'd be like real sisters forever. And this man has wounded her terribly. He reached inside her, drew out her heart, held it for a while in the palm of his hand, and then crushed it. I couldn't care less about his side of the story.

I look at Pearl. She is staring straight ahead, and her face is a little dazed and innocent like a child's. After a few moments she emerges from her reverie and meets my eyes.

"At least I have memories now," she says. "That may not sound like a lot to you, but to me it's everything. It's enough. I don't need anything else."

These words sound strangely familiar to me—I am sure I have heard them somewhere before, yet I can't place where. And then I remember. These are the exact same words that Auntie Bella spoke to us all a few days after Uncle Harry died. During the *shiva*, in the living room downstairs. We didn't believe her then, a woman of only forty-eight (just seven years older than I am now), and still attractive. But she made good her word, and never married again. She turned her back on the world, with the exception of family, a few old friends, and a sculpture class every three or four years, and holed herself up with Pearl, just the two of them, mother and daughter, in that dark, poky little house. I look closely at Pearl for some sign of awareness, but she looks back at me simply and directly, apparently oblivious that the words she has spoken are not her own. Then her expression deepens—she's gazing at me with a very clear, steady look, and for some reason I can't help thinking how beautiful she is.

"I'm never going out again," she says. "Not even downstairs, if people are there. I don't want to see anybody, I don't want everyone staring at me."

"Staring at you?" I say. "They care about you, Pearl, they just want to...comfort—"

"I don't want their comfort," snaps Pearl. "I want to be left alone."

For a few moments I don't say anything. Then I say stiffly:

"You have been effective, I think, in communicating this."

Pearl absorbs this for a bit, and then, with a wry smile, nods.

Outside the window, it is indigo now—no longer the pale blue dusk that it was just minutes ago. Even as I watch, the blue becomes deeper and darker, ever-thickening like a dangerous fog—yet so beautiful that all I can think of is its beauty. I stare mesmerized at the fast descending night.

I'm startled by a sound: the sound of a voice. I tear my eyes away from the window and shift them back towards Pearl. Simultaneously the sounds that I heard replay themselves in my head, and gradually they begin to take on meaning: "I miss my mother." "I miss my mother" is what Pearl said. But I'm sure I must have heard her wrong, because her face now, as I look at it, is totally without expression. As if she hasn't spoken at all.

She starts to cry. I hesitate; then I edge forward on the bed and put my arms around her. She doesn't push me away, though her body stays stiff. She feels very bony and frail. All of a sudden she relaxes against me, and for a moment rests her head on my shoulder. Then she sits back, with dignity wiping her eyes.

"You'd better go back down," she says.

I nod, but I don't move. I'm not ready to leave her yet. Though now I'm starting to feel that I'd better go down soon. Otherwise, I too could get stuck in this room, in this little world of Pearl's that I have too perfectly entered, that has started to actually make sense to me. I said I wanted to understand, and now I do. But what difference has that made? Nothing has changed. Pearl is still Pearl, her future the same cul-de-sac that it was before I walked up the stairs. And it hasn't done anything for me, either. On the contrary, I have never felt worse than I do right now—I actually feel physically unwell: breathless and dizzy, with a growing constriction in my chest. I wonder if I'm having a heart attack.

No, I answer myself, as if I am my own doctor. *This isn't a heart attack. This is sorrow. Just sorrow, don't be afraid.* And I tighten my lips so I will not cry.

Pearl is looking at me shrewdly. "You go downstairs," she directs me, "and you tell them…" And now I am the younger cousin again, I am being sent on an errand, and dismissed, and it is a great relief. "You tell them from me," she says, "that I don't need any of their help. I just want this house. This house is mine, she gave this house to me." (She says these words, but I can hear her singing them instead, to the tune of "Exodus": *This land is mine, God gave this land to me*—we saw that movie together when it first came out, thirty-something years ago.)

"Other than that," she continues, "I just want to be left alone. Tell them not to bother me. I can order food by phone. I can even order from the drug store by phone. And I can send away through the mail for panties and nightgowns when I need new stuff. We got a catalogue from Sears a few months ago. They have everything there—even shoes, pots and pans..."

I stare at her.

She looks right back. "And if I get sick," she says (answering the last of the family's questions, as if she has read its collective mind), "Auntie Dorothy is just next door. I'll ask for help if I need it."

I can't conceal my dismay. "But Pearl..." I say.

"Don't worry," she says calmly (and now *she* is the comforter, comforting *me*). "I'm not going to do anything stupid. And I've got everything figured out, how to manage. You can see that for yourself."

Yes, I can. I can see it all perfectly. My cousin is going to spend the rest of her life alone in this room, nine feet by twelve, with the four walls reaching straight up to the ceiling—and the ceiling sealing the sky out and her in, like the cover of a cardboard box closing over a guinea pig. She might as well be buried here alive.

"And there's always Dial-A-Doctor," Pearl is saying in a cheery, practical tone of voice, "like if I fall or something. So Auntie Dorothy doesn't have to 'look in on' me all the time. We've never gotten along anyway. She never liked me, she never believed me, she always thought I was just making everything up."

Pearl pauses, frowns, and for a moment studies me. "*You* believed me, though," she says. "*You* understood. Didn't you?"

I can't speak. I'm afraid I'll cry. I nod my head.

Pearl frowns again. Then she gazes at me pensively for quite some time. A long, deep look.

"You were my best friend," she says.

I look down. My head is bowed, as if I am receiving a blessing from someone, from a dying person. Or two: It feels like a double blessing—a goodbye not only from Pearl, but also from Auntie Bella.

"Well," I say, "not a very good one," and burst into tears. "I'm sorry," I sob. "I never, really...I never...like...with Expo—"

And I sob convulsively, brokenly, unable to stem the waves of regret and grief welling up in me and spilling out, over and over again. With my hands I cover my face, which is wet and slippery now, almost rubbery, as if my face has somehow become a mask. Something tickles the corner of my mouth. *A tear. It must be a tear.* Automatically my tongue darts out like a snake's, and tastes it—a habit from childhood, to see if it's salty (salty tears mean your sadness is real). Yes. It is.

And with my eyes covered, I can now see clearly: Auntie Bella in front of her house twenty-six years ago, a woman of forty-six tending her roses. She was bending over a yellow rosebush, wearing her earth-stained gardening gloves, and clipping away the dead branches and leaves with a big pair of shears. I stopped to say hi. I was on my way home from school, grade ten, my arms full of books. I didn't feel burdened, though, none of it was homework. It was the last day of school and the next day was the beginning of summer vacation. It was a warm and beautiful June day, and Auntie Bella came over to where I was standing, her pruning shears still in hand. Briefly we talked, me on the sidewalk and her at the edge of the grass. We talked about Expo—what else?—Expo being short for Exposition '67, the International

World's Fair taking place that year in Montreal. It had just opened the weekend before, it was on everybody's lips—no one talked about anything else—and the city was bursting with tourists and with pride. I hadn't been there yet, neither had Auntie Bella, but she'd heard from Henny Wolfson that it surpassed all expectations, it was like a magical world, something you couldn't even imagine until you'd been there. My mother had been once already, so had my cousin Howie and a girl I knew from school. I told Auntie Bella I was going the next day. She asked with who. I told her. "Well, some other time," she said, "please take Pearl. She's dying to go, but you know her, she'll never go by herself. She'll only go if somebody takes her." "Okay," I said. "Sure." And then to my surprise, Auntie Bella's face turned hopeful, opening up before my eyes like a rose.

I went to Expo three times in the next few weeks. Once with my parents and some friends of theirs who were visiting from Chicago and had a daughter my age. Once on a trip organized by my school. And once I took a lift there and back with my cousin Michael, and walked around by myself while he looked at all the science exhibits. When I wasn't at Expo, though, I didn't have much to do. Mostly I hung around the house, being bored. One day, about three weeks into July, on a day so slow and dead you could hear the flies buzz, I wandered into the backyard, and there all of a sudden was Pearl. Our backyards were communal, hers and ours and Auntie Dorothy's, they all ran together into one long stretch; and each year at the end of the summer, we had a barbecue there for the whole family, with all the aunts and uncles and cousins eating hamburgers and corn on the cob, and watermelon for dessert. I was surprised to bump into her, and it was awkward between us: We had barely seen each other since our confrontation the month before about me going to my class party, "selling out" and all that. She asked me if I'd been to Expo yet. I shrugged and said—quoting my mother—that I'd been a few times, but I hated the long lines; I probably wasn't going to go again until all the tourists were gone, since after Labour Day I'd be able to get into everything with no waits at all. Pearl shrugged and acted like she didn't care. This was on a Wednesday, a day so hot that in the late afternoon Auntie Bella came out into the backyard, and stood frowning over her tomatoes, worrying that they would scorch.

On Saturday morning, around eleven, Pearl looked out of her living room window and saw me and Hindy Horowitz walking past her house. Our street was a dead end: To get from my house to anywhere, you had to walk past Auntie Dorothy's, past Pearl's, and then another block and a half to the main street that led out from our neighbourhood, and connected us to the rest of the city. So just 'cause Hindy and I were walking past Pearl's house didn't mean anything at all. We could have been going anywhere. To a movie. To the shopping centre. Bowling.

But you could always tell when someone was going to Expo. In addition to looking like a tourist (the big, floppy hat necessary against the summer sun, and the obligatory camera and canteen), you also carried, if you were smart, a little fold-up stool to sit on while you waited to get into the exhibits. The Czech pavilion, for example, was an hour-and-a-half wait; Cominco, Kaleidoscope, and Trinidad Tobago & Grenada were all two hours at least. Pearl saw me walking with my little fold-up stool—it was made of aluminum and orangey-red canvas, you could spot it easily a half a block away—and there was no question whatsoever about where Hindy and I were going. There was also no question that I was trying to sneak away without being seen. Why else would I have looked up anxiously, guiltily, at her living room window as we passed her house?

Pearl saw, and immediately understood. I looked up, and our eyes met only for a moment, but that was enough to see how hurt and shocked she was. Her face looked slightly dazed, as if she had been stabbed in the back—was even bleeding profusely from the wound—but didn't quite believe it yet. Hindy Horowitz kept on talking, oblivious, chattering on and on about something or other. She talked all the way to the bus stop, and then once we were on the bus, all the way to Expo; and when we got there, she talked as we waited in lines, and walked through pavilions, and ate, and came back home. She talked and talked and talked. I don't remember a word she said. For the entire time, a clammy, sickening feeling gripped my stomach: a mixture of guilt, shame, and fear. I felt as if Pearl's head, the only part of her I could see in the window, was sitting decapitated in the pit of my stomach. All day long, I saw nothing of Expo. All I saw was that face, that terrible face, as if some Gothic spirit had come to haunt me.

But I did get in with the cool kids, as I'd hoped to, by sucking up to Hindy Horowitz and inviting her to come with me to Expo. I didn't need to be popular, like her—I didn't consider this, really, even within the realm of possibility; I just wanted to be normal. To be part of the group at school, instead of on the fringe—to have some friends to hang around with, instead of only Pearl (so dark, and intense, always talking about "the wretched of the earth"). I wanted to be invited to join in when they went shopping on Saturday afternoons (even though I didn't like shopping). To be let in on the gossip (even though I didn't like gossip). I didn't even like *them* very much, but I desperately wanted them to like *me*. And I succeeded. Hindy thought my silence that day was cool and mysterious, and she and the other girls, when talking it over in the weeks that followed, couldn't understand why they'd never noticed me before. They began including me some of the time, and they taught me how to dress, and then once I was going out with Bobby Zuker, I was as "in" as I'd wanted to be. And actually I've stayed in touch with most of them ever since. A lot of us ended up living not far from each other in Toronto. They may not be the smartest, most interesting people in the world, but they're not stupid, either, and they mean well. Hindy's husband, for example—she married an architect—connected Mike to one of his biggest clients. I wouldn't say they're our "friends" exactly, like Pearl and I were friends. I've never again had a friend like that. But we go out to dinner together in couples once or twice a year. We carpool our kids. We help each other out if we can. Normal stuff.

So that day at Expo I got what I wanted. But at a price—look how I wounded Pearl. Look at what I did. "It was an accident," I feel like telling her. "Like dropping a glass on the floor." But as my mother used to say whenever that would happen, it doesn't matter whether it's an accident or not. It's shattered now into a million little pieces, and you can't put them back together. That's what matters: You can never make it whole again.

Stupid, anyway, these things from childhood. Stupid, silly, at the age of forty-one, to think that my slighting Pearl, not inviting her to Expo one day in a summer long ago, could have had a significant effect on her, turned her into a hermit, ended her life. What hubris. What power. When Auntie Bella suggested it, seven, maybe eight years ago, I laughed in her face. We were sitting in a Chinese restaurant, I was back in Montreal briefly for a conference, and had taken her out for lunch just "to get her out of the house." And there she was, after her egg rolls and before her chow mein, twisting away at her handkerchief, and going on and on and on about Pearl, a litany as predictable and as automatically recited as a series of Hail Marys (her handkerchief could have been a rosary the way she fingered it). Just to interrupt her and break the monologue,

I asked her what *Pearl* thought about it all—why *she* thought she never left the house, what *she* thought had happened to her. How did *she* understand it from *her* point of view?

"Oh, you know Pearl," Auntie Bella said with a laugh. "If she isn't blaming one person, she's blaming another. If it isn't my fault, it's yours..."

"Mine?!" I exclaimed.

"Oh, this is her latest thing," said Auntie Bella. "She says you dropped her in high school. You didn't take her to Expo one day, you went with somebody else...Do I know? She thinks if you had stayed her friend, instead of getting in with Hindy Horowitz and all that crowd, who knows? Maybe—"

I laughed in shocked amazement. "What!" I said to Auntie Bella. "You don't really believe...?!"

My aunt's eyes wandered away from me, and she gave a philosophical shrug. "Do I know?" she asked. "I don't know what to believe. If it wasn't that, anyway, it would probably have been something else. We'll never know. But anyway, never mind. Don't pay any attention..."

I stared at her, dumbfounded. And just as I was beginning to pull myself together to respond, we were interrupted by the chow mein. There was the usual flurry around welcoming food. We had to make room for it on the table, and we had to say how good it looked and smelled. The waiter insisted that we taste it, right then and there, in front of him, which we did—and he grinned with delight when we praised it. He left and we ate. And the conversation shifted naturally to lighter topics, like Chinese restaurants in Montreal. We never returned to this matter again.

"Here," says Pearl, and something blue enters my field of vision. A box of kleenex. I remove my hands from my face, and pull out some tissues without looking up. I wipe my eyes and cheeks and blow my nose. Then, looking at the box, I say, "I'm sorry, Pearl. I'm so sorry." I want to say more, but I'm on the verge of tears again, and I'm afraid I'll once more start crying.

There is silence. Then I hear Pearl's voice. "I know you are."

I look up. Her eyes are drier than mine, and less puffy for sure, but just as sad. And yet they are not unkind. We look at each other for a long, steady moment. Then Pearl says gently, "You really should go back down now."

I nod, and say "Yes." I get off the bed and stand facing her. "Goodbye," I say.

Pearl gets up then, too, and comes over to me. She kisses me very softly, like a butterfly resting, once on each cheek. I'm surprised by the second kiss: I'd forgotten they kiss French-style here in Montreal. I kiss her back on both cheeks, too.

"Say hello from me," she says.

"I will."

"Bye," says Pearl.

"Bye."

I shut the door behind me when I leave.

I start down the stairs. And then on the fourth step I stop. One or two more steps and the staircase will curve, and the family seated together in the living room will be able to see me coming down, with my face all blotchy. And then there will be no turning back. I'll get to the bottom, they'll ask me what happened, and I'll have to tell them. But I have no idea what to say. I pause on the stairs, compose myself, and think for a moment. I decide to tell them that there is no question at all of Pearl living anywhere except in this house. This house is hers, Auntie Bella left it to her, and she would never even consider any other possibility. I'll also tell them that, in my professional opinion, Pearl is perfectly capable of living on her own and taking care of herself. And I'll tell them about the plans she's made for managing her daily life.

But I won't tell them anything real. Like how she really feels about them. Or about what happened with Ricky. Even if she'd said I could, I would never be able to explain to them, in terms they could understand, how one year ago, Pearl was born— brought to life sexually and emotionally by a man who loved her—and then, within three months, virtually destroyed by this same man. They would just roll their eyes and laugh at her. And at me, too, for taking her seriously, for taking her side. And suddenly I don't want to go down there. Not just "not yet." But not at all. I don't belong there with them. Then again, I don't belong with Pearl, either. I don't know where I belong. Maybe nowhere—just going up and down this staircase for the rest of my life. Like the angel on Jacob's ladder, going back and forth eternally between heaven and the earth.

~